Jamie stopped at the top of the ridge and looked over all the cabins until she found hers, in time to see her parents and Jeremy come running out to greet the Mitchells, who had just arrived.

Jamie knew they'd all have hamburgers and chili dogs for dinner, and everybody would laugh and swap stories about past summers—about the time she and Todd got "lost" sixty yards from the cabins when they were five. The last thing she wanted to do was join them.

The sun was getting really low now, and there was almost no one on the lake. But at the end of the pier, she saw a tallish blond boy, and even though she couldn't see his face, she knew who he was.

He was the boy she'd just seen in the drugstore. He was the one with the dimples and the blue eyes, the one who suddenly wasn't a dream anymore, but was actually alive, and here, at the same lake where Jamie was going to spend five wonderful weeks....

Heart to Heart

Summer to Summer

CAROL ELLIS

BALLANTINE BOOKS • NEW YORK

RLI: $\dfrac{\text{VL: 5 + up}}{\text{IL: 6 + up}}$

Library of Congress Catalog Card Number: 84-91158

ISBN 0-345-31631-2

Manufactured in the United States of America

First Edition: February 1985

Book One

Jamie at Fourteen

☀ One ☀

"Well," Jamie's mother said, "it hasn't changed a bit."

Jamie had been waiting for that line ever since they set foot in the cabin fifteen minutes before. Jamie wasn't in the same room with her mother, but even so, she knew exactly how her mother looked. Audrey Watson was standing in the middle of the tiny kitchen with her hands on her hips. She was gazing around at the knotty-pine walls, the cracked blue linoleum, and the bottled-gas stove that looked as if it belonged in an old western movie. She was trying to frown, but she couldn't. Jamie's mother was happy to be on vacation, happy to be in the same mountain-lake cabin that she'd been coming to for ten years, and she was secretly glad that it hadn't changed a bit.

Jamie, on the other hand, wasn't so glad. Not that life back home in Denver was all that exciting, but *she'd* been coming on vacation to Sunrise Lake for ten years, too, since she was four years old. As far as she was concerned, a little change wouldn't hurt. She'd hinted that there were other places to go on vacation—California or the Gulf of Mexico, to name two—but her parents hardly listened. They said they couldn't afford Jamie's idea of a vacation, but Jamie knew the real reason was that they just didn't want to go anywhere new.

Jamie was standing in her "bedroom," which was about five feet square. It had a metal cot for her sleeping bag, an old blanket draped between it and the kitchen, and another blanket hanging over the closet door. Next to her room was the bathroom, with its rippled tin shower stall, and on the other side of that was her parents' bedroom. The walls dividing them stopped about two feet short of the ceiling, but Jamie was thankful she had *some* privacy at least and didn't have to sleep on the living room couch, like her brother Jeremy. But then Jeremy was only nine years old and didn't care about privacy yet.

She heard a cupboard door squeak in the kitchen, and then her mother laughed. "Guess what's still here?"

"The old rattle I made to scare away the bears," Jamie said. Her mother said *that* every summer, too.

"Imagine. Nobody's thrown it away all these years."

"Umm." Jamie was staring at the inside wall of her closet where she'd written "Watson Was Here" in red magic marker the summer she was ten. That was when she was a Sherlock Holmes freak and wanted to be a great detective. Now she had no idea what she wanted to be, except maybe older, or at least different.

She heard a loud noise and jumped. Her mother was behind her, shaking the bear rattle, which was an empty "family size" pork and beans can filled with rocks and pieces of broken chain. Jamie had sprayed it black and printed the words "Bear Scare" on it. She used to put it on top of the garbage can outside the cabin, and if a bear came foraging for food at night, the rattle was supposed to send it packing. She'd watch through her bedroom window, ready to shine her flashlight into some grizzly bear's eyes, when the rattle fell off the can. She'd never seen a bear, but the rattle had sent hundreds of porcupines and raccoons scurrying for the woods. It also woke her parents up so often that they made her put it away.

"Didn't Todd help you make this?" her mother asked. Todd Mitchell was Jamie's age. His family rented the cabin next door during the same five July weeks that the Watsons came to the lake. "I seem to remember you two discussing it for hours before you finally unveiled the finished product."

"It was Todd's idea," Jamie said. "But I made it work. He actually wanted to catch a stupid bear and sell it to the circus."

"That's right. Todd always has the big schemes, doesn't he? You're the more practical one."

"Umm."

"Jamie?"

"What?"

"You're not coming down with something, I hope." Mrs. Watson stuck out a hand and felt Jamie's forehead. "You were awfully quiet on the way up here."

"I'm fine, Mom." Jamie pulled the blanket aside, went into the kitchen, and sat in one of the four unmatching chairs. She wasn't fine, but since she didn't know exactly what was wrong, she thought she ought to keep quiet about it. "Riding in a car for six hours makes me hot and itchy, that's all." She decided to change the subject. "What's taking Daddy and the Germ so long? I'm starving."

Mrs. Watson started unloading a sack of groceries. "You don't have to wait for them to eat." She tossed Jamie an apple. "That should hold you."

"Thanks."

"Anyway, you know your father. He'll inspect every boat with a magnifying glass, as if he were planning to buy a yacht instead of just renting a rowboat." She laughed. "He and Jeremy are probably on the lake right now, making sure the one they picked is seaworthy."

Jamie took a big bite of apple. "How come the Germ always gets to do the fun things?" she mumbled.

Her mother raised her eyebrows. "As I recall, your father asked both Jeremy *and* you to come along. You said no, Jamie." She took an apple for herself. "Why don't you join them? Or take a walk, go find out the swimming-test schedule? Maybe you'll run into some people your own age, and you can all be grumpy together."

Jamie started to claim that she wasn't grumpy, which was a lie, but just then the cabin door opened and her father and brother came inside. They both smelled of fishing bait.

"Hey!" Bob Watson was a big man with a big voice, and when he was excited, as he was then, he bellowed like a giant. Jamie always had trouble picturing him teaching economics, because she knew it didn't give him much of a chance to bellow. "Larry down at the docks says the trout are biting like mosquitoes! Not just in the lake but in the streams, too." He took a crusted iron frying pan out of the cupboard and set it on the stove. "We're going to be eating high on the hog this summer!"

"That's a nice mix of metaphors." Jamie's mother was a teacher, too, of eighth-grade English.

"Wait'll you see the boat we got," Jeremy said. "It's neat!"

"They're all alike," Jamie said.

"They are not. Some of them are blue, and some are gray."

6

Jamie tossed her apple core into an empty sack. "And they stink from all the fish people have caught in them."

"Stink?" Mr. Watson looked insulted. "Fish don't stink. They smell terrific. Especially trout."

"Not until they're cooked," Jamie said.

Her father laughed. "Well, how do you plan to get past that problem when you're catching them?"

"Yeah, dummy," the Germ said. "You going to wear a clothespin on your nose?"

"Jeremy." Mrs. Watson gave him a look. "No ugly names, please."

"Maybe I just won't fish," Jamie said. "Dummy."

"Jamie!"

"Not fish?" Now her father looked hurt. "Jamie, you're my best fishing partner. You're even better than your mother, and that's saying a lot." He patted Jeremy on the shoulder. "No offense, Jeremy, but we've been at it longer than you have." He turned back to Jamie. "You're not serious, I hope."

Jamie shook her head. "I'll fish with you, Daddy; don't worry."

"Well, try not to make it sound like a punishment. I want you to enjoy it. You always did before."

Jamie's mother sighed and started rummaging around in the groceries again. "Jamie's just tired from the ride," she said. "I think we all are. Let's have a snack and then go exploring."

"I'm not hungry anymore." Jamie stood up. "I think I'll hike into Spruce, if it's okay with everybody."

"It's fine with *me*," Jeremy said.

Jamie saw her mother and father exchange looks. They both raised their eyebrows and shrugged at each other. Then her mother said, "All right. But don't be too long, please. The Mitchells should be here soon, and we'll all have dinner together." She handed Jamie her wallet. "Get me a bottle of hand lotion, if you would, please. I forgot to pack mine. And spend the rest on something for yourself." She smiled.

"Thanks, Mom." Jamie knew her mother was trying to be nice and ignore her "grumpiness," so she smiled back and forced herself not to edge toward the door. "I'll be back later, okay?"

"Stay on the trail," her mother warned.

"And put some sunscreen on your face," her father said. "You don't want to burn up the first day you're here."

Jamie went into the bathroom, smeared some sunscreen on her nose and cheeks, promised she wouldn't wander off into the woods, told Jeremy she'd bring him a comic book if she had enough money left, and finally managed to get away.

It was about three o'clock in the afternoon, and the sun was still hot. Their cabin was only about thirty yards from Sunrise Lake, but Jamie ignored that path and took another one, which led her into the woods. She felt better as soon as she stepped into the shade of the pine and aspen trees, but she knew that feeling wouldn't last long. Lately, it seemed that she always wanted to get away from her family, but about ten minutes after she did, she felt worse than ever.

The trail to Spruce was wide and well-worn; she didn't know why her parents were always so worried about letting her go alone. It was only a twenty-minute walk, and you didn't even need hiking boots.

It was more of a garden path than a mountain trail, but Jamie pushed along as if she were a pioneer, not almost a freshman from Denver. That was something she always did—pretend. Her mother said she was the practical one, and it was true in a way, but Jamie had dreams, too, like

8

being a famous detective or a lawyer or the first freshman in the history of her high school to be prom queen.

She grabbed an aspen leaf and twirled it around in her fingers, trying to make it quake the way it did on the tree. She wouldn't mind being a scientist someday. Four summers ago, she and Todd Mitchell found a dead rabbit and spent two days convincing each other they could bring it back to life before they finally gave up. It would be nice to know how to save things from dying. It would also be nice to invent a way to get rid of pale skin or a way to keep her hair blonde all over all year instead of just bleached on the ends from the summer sun and plain brown the rest of the time. She'd thought of trying a rinse, but she knew the Germ would notice immediately and make some sarcastic remark, plus her father would put his foot down, and her mother would say "absolutely not."

The way she looked bothered her a lot. Sometimes she felt too fat, and other times she felt too thin. Sometimes she wished her legs were longer, like a model's, and other times she was afraid she'd never stop growing. And it seemed as if her clothes were either too tight or too loose. In fact, she never felt quite "right," which added to her grumpiness.

"Stop worrying about it," Carrie always said. Carrie Donovan was her best friend back home. "You've got great blue eyes and nice legs. Just be yourself."

Jamie tossed the aspen leaf down and laughed out loud. Carrie had curly black hair, dark brown eyes, a perfect complexion, and a brain that didn't stop. She could get by on her looks *or* her mind any day.

She'd asked Jamie to stay at her house instead of going to the lake that summer, but Jamie knew her parents wouldn't let her. Besides, Carrie was getting awfully popular lately. She'd probably get invited to a lot of parties that summer. And if Jamie had stayed with her, she'd have had to choose between tagging along where she wasn't really wanted and staying at home and playing chess with Carrie's little sister, who was also a "brain" and usually won.

Jamie crossed a log bridge and followed the trail down into the town of Spruce. Its main street had a post office, a restaurant for tourists and campers who were sick of trout, and a drugstore. She headed for the drugstore.

Mr. Taylor, the owner, knew her by name. "Jamie Watson! Welcome back. What can I get for you?"

"Hi, Mr. Taylor." Jamie looked around. Nothing had changed there, either. "My mother needs some hand lotion."

"Jergens." He reached underneath the counter and pulled out a glass bottle covered with dust. "The only kind." He winked. "The only kind I carry, anyway."

Jamie laughed, the way she always did. Then she strolled around, trying to find something for herself. She didn't wear makeup yet, and the only magazines were on movie stars or fly-fishing. She found a Jedi comic for Jeremy and finally settled on some after-shower splash for herself. It was supposed to make her smell like lemons, and she figured that would go well with trout.

She was still browsing around, looking for a good paperback or even a book of crossword puzzles, when the bell on the door jangled. A minute later, she heard a voice say, "Not much to choose from, is there?"

Jamie glanced up and into the bluest eyes she'd ever seen. They were bluer even than Sunrise Lake, and they belonged to a boy that her friend Carrie would have called "gorgeous." He was slim and tanned, with curly blond hair on his arms and legs. The hair on his head was thick and sandy. And when he smiled at her, she saw two of the most adorable dimples she'd ever laid eyes on.

10

He smiled at her again, then turned his blue eyes to the rack of suntan lotions. Jamie told herself to stop standing there with her mouth hanging open, but for a while she just couldn't help it. Finally, she got up the strength to pay Mr. Taylor and left the store.

Her cheeks felt hot even though it was beginning to cool off outside, and she knew why. Boys were another thing that had been on her mind lately. Every time she saw one who was even halfway interesting-looking, it took her all of five minutes to work up an entire fantasy about how they got together, fell in love, and spent hours holding hands and going on one date after another. Somehow, in her fantasies, she always managed to be suddenly beautiful. Her hair didn't hang like limp shoelaces, and her body was long and lean. And she was incredibly witty.

Mostly, though, she concentrated on the boy. She'd taken things she liked about everyone who ever caught her eye and turned them all into an impossibly handsome boy with sandy-blond hair, dimples, and a hypnotizing voice. What she'd never expected was that her favorite dream would step out of her mind and into the Spruce drugstore.

She wasn't surprised at all, though, that she hadn't been able to think of anything to say. This was reality, not fantasy, and in reality she was fourteen years old, with absolutely no experience to her name.

By the time Jamie got back to the lake, the sun was starting to dip behind the mountains in the west. She stopped at the top of the ridge and looked over all the cabins until she found hers, in time to see her parents and Jeremy come running out to greet the Mitchells, who had just arrived. They looked wrinkled and stiff from driving all the way from Kansas, but Jamie knew they were smiling.

She saw the grown-ups hug and shake hands, and she watched Todd and his little brother Dave start talking to Jeremy as though they were year-round neighbors instead of just summer ones.

She couldn't hear them, but she knew her father was talking about all the fish they were going to catch and that her mother was telling everybody about the new hiking boots she just bought.

Jamie knew they'd have hamburgers and chili dogs for dinner, and everybody would laugh and catch up on a year's news and swap stories about past vacations—about the time she and Todd got "lost" sixty yards from the cabins when they were five, for instance. And all of a sudden, the last thing in the world she wanted to do was join in.

Unfortunately, she was still wearing the bright yellow sweatshirt she'd put on that morning, so it was pretty hard to disappear, even if she'd had a place to disappear to.

Her mother spotted her and waved frantically with both hands, as if there were a swarm of mosquitoes two feet above her head. Jamie waved back with one hand and started shuffling down the trail, scattering little pebbles with her scruffy sneakers.

The sun was really getting low then, and there was almost no one on the lake. She glanced at the rocky beach, which was roped off for swimmers. It was empty. But at the end of the pier, she saw a tallish blond boy standing alone with his hands on his hips, staring out at the blue-green water. His back was to Jamie, and even though she couldn't read the letters on his crimson sweatshirt, she knew what they spelled: "Sunrise Lake Lifeguard."

And even though she couldn't see his face, she knew who he was. He was the boy from the drugstore. He was the one with the dimples and the blue eyes, the one who suddenly wasn't a dream anymore but was actually alive—and there, at the same lake where Jamie was going to spend five wonderful weeks.

☀ *Two* ☀

*D*ear Jamie,

   How's the lake? Wet, I'll bet, ha-ha. Are you getting a great tan?

Jamie looked up from Carrie's letter and crossed her eyes. When she did that, she could see the blob of sunscreen glistening on her nose. At that rate, she'd never be able to get a great tan, which her mother said was bad for the skin, anyway. Even if her skin was the tanning type, it wouldn't have mattered during the first week of vacation. The lake had been wet, all right, and so had everything else, because it had rained half the time. And when it wasn't raining that week, it was still cloudy and cold.

"You'd think this was April instead of July," her father kept muttering. Everybody was touchy, and Jamie decided it was because no one had expected to spend so

14

much time indoors with everyone else. They'd played a lot of Scrabble and chess when it was raining, and when it wasn't, they'd bundled up and hiked around the muddy trails. The fish weren't biting, and swimming was out of the question.

Finally, though, the sun had come out, and now Jamie was with her father and Jeremy, sitting in the rowboat and waiting for another jerk on the line. It was seven-thirty in the morning; they'd been out for an hour and caught three fish. Her father wanted one more, he said, so they could all have trout for breakfast.

"Look alive, Jamie," he said. "If your brother or I get a bite, we'll need a steady hand."

"Don't worry, Dad. I'll be ready." Jamie hadn't wanted to fish, so she'd volunteered to scoop them out of the water with the net. Her father and Jeremy kept casting and reeling, never taking their eyes from the sparkling blue water. They looked slightly bored, but Jamie knew that mentally they had their fingers crossed. She yawned, shifted around on the hard wooden seat, and went back to Carrie's letter.

I'll bet you're surprised to be hearing from me before I've even heard from you, but I wanted to tell you about the party. Remember? The one at Diane's house the night you left.

Jamie remembered. She'd really wanted to go, which didn't help her mood on the drive to the lake.

It was so much fun. I wish you could have come. Remember Diane told us her cousin was visiting? Well, he was at the party, naturally, and he's gorgeous! Too bad he lives in Colorado Springs, but he'll be here for two more weeks, and Diane said she'd make sure to bring him swimming every day. He's sixteen, so I guess he probably likes older girls, but there's nothing he can do about that while he's stuck here! It's too bad you're gone—

15

we could have had a great time talking about him, because he's just our type.

Jamie smiled. She and Carrie had the same taste in boys, so she figured Diane's cousin must be cute.

But maybe you've already met somebody. Are there lots of good-looking boys up there?

Jamie folded the letter and stuffed it in the pocket of her jeans. There may have been lots of good-looking boys at the lake, but there was only one she cared about. The problem was, she'd hardly seen him since that first day in Spruce. How could you get to know a lifeguard when you couldn't go swimming?

Once she saw him walking along the lakefront in the rain, his sweatshirt hood covering his blond hair. He looked as bored and lonely as she felt, and she had an immediate fantasy about going out and joining him. She imagined them walking toward each other and smiling, the only two people by the lake in the rain. Then she lost her courage and played Monopoly with her family instead. She didn't see him for days after that, and she started thinking she might never see him again if the weather didn't break.

Finally, though, the sun came out and it was the first day for swimming. At eleven o'clock, all the kids under sixteen had to swim to a raft a little way out in the lake to prove they were good enough to swim alone. It didn't matter if you'd qualified the summer before; you still had to do it. Jamie had been swimming to that raft since she was seven. For the last seven summers she'd thought it was a stupid rule, but this summer she didn't mind at all. In fact, she couldn't wait. He was a lifeguard. He'd be there watching her swim. So who cared if her father and brother caught another fish?

"Okay, Jer, okay!" her father whispered. "You've hooked one. Just take it nice and easy. Reel in, slowly, slowly."

16

Jamie looked at Jeremy's line. It was drawn tight, and when he pulled at the pole, it curved in on itself until it was bent nearly in half.

"Pull . . . reel," her father was saying. "Okay, okay, pull. No, not so hard! It's a big one, so you're going to have to outwit it."

"I didn't know fish had wits," Jamie mumbled.

"Just a figure of speech." Mr. Watson kept his eyes on the line. "Got the net?"

"Umm." Jamie sighed.

Jeremy let out a whoop of excitement. He looked ready to hop up and down.

"Steady, Jer," his father said. "You've got to concentrate. This one's a fighter, but it'll get tired before you do. Just play along with it until it doesn't have any fight left. Then you'll have it right where you want it—in the frying pan."

Jeremy nodded, but Jamie said, "That sounds cruel."

Jeremy looked disgusted. "When did you start feeling sorry for fish?"

Jamie shrugged. She didn't know when. Right then there were three trout in the creel, and she'd put them there. Even with their rainbow stripes, they weren't exactly lovable-looking. And until this summer, she'd enjoyed fishing. She didn't know why it bothered her then. She shrugged again. "It just doesn't seem fair, that's all."

"Hah." Jeremy's cheeks were pink. "Tell me all about it the next time you eat a hamburger."

Mr. Watson shook his head. "Look. We've hooked a fish. Why don't we just land it and discuss the moral aspects of the whole procedure some other time?"

In spite of her feelings, Jamie netted the fish, took the hook out of its mouth, and plopped it in the creel like an expert. It was the biggest catch of the morning. Jeremy was beaming, and Jamie congratulated him, mostly to keep peace but also because he would have been terribly hurt if she hadn't. If she didn't like hurting fish, how could she hurt her brother's feelings? She patted him on the back and decided to eat Cheerios for breakfast.

"Jamie?"

"What?"

"Todd's here. He says hurry up."

"Okay, Mom. Tell him I'll be out in a minute."

"What's taking you so long? You've been in there for half an hour." Jamie heard her mother take a step closer to the bathroom. "Are you sick?"

"No, I'm not sick! I'll be out in just a minute."

Jamie waited until she heard her mother walk back into the kitchen, then climbed off the short wooden stool. What she'd been doing for the last half hour was putting on her new swimsuit and trying to get a good look at herself in the bathroom's dinky mirror. Standing on the floor, she could see herself from about the chest up. The suit was a one-piece in a violet-blue color, with extra-thin straps that crisscrossed in the back all the way down to below her waist. There wasn't much she could do about her short, straight hair except tuck it behind her ears, but she thought the color of her suit made her eyes stand out.

She climbed up on the stool again for another chest-down view. Her knees were a little knobby, but her legs were long, and she figured a lifeguard might appreciate them.

She hopped down, put some lemon-scented splash on her shoulders and neck, and took a last look. She wasn't bad; she just wasn't spectacular. At least she was a good swimmer.

When she walked into the kitchen, her mother looked up from a cup of tea. "Jamie, where on earth did you get that suit?"

18

"At the mall, the day before we left. With my baby-sitting money."

"Why didn't you show it to me?"

"You didn't ask to see it." Jamie turned around and tried to sound casual. "What do you think?"

"Well." Mrs. Watson looked her up and down. "It's a far cry from your black tank suit." She sipped some tea. "I just hope you put plenty of lotion on your lower back—there's absolutely no protection down there."

Jamie sighed. "I knew you'd hate it."

"I do not hate it. It's a lovely suit. I just think it's a little ... mature for you." Mrs. Watson smiled. "The blue's nice with your eyes."

"Thanks."

"It's a good thing this is a lake and not the ocean. The waves would tear that thing off of you in two seconds flat."

"Well, it *is* a lake, Mother."

Jamie grabbed her towel and stepped out onto the sloping, screened-in porch. Todd Mitchell was standing at the screen, looking intently across the lake. Without turning around, he said, "Have you seen the lantern yet?"

Jamie didn't have to ask what he was talking about. There was a haunted cabin at Sunrise Lake. Actually, it was just a deserted, crumbling hut set at the spot where the lake narrowed and curved out of sight behind a bunch of hills, but everybody—all the kids, anyway—was sure it was haunted. The legend was that Ben Tyler, a fur trapper in the eighteen hundreds, had starved to death in that cabin one awful winter and that his ghost still went out at night, searching for food.

You couldn't see the cabin from the Watsons' porch, but you could see the bend in the lake, and Jamie and Todd had seen Tyler's bobbing lantern fifteen times, which was a record. During her detective period, Jamie had had

19

great dreams of solving the mystery. Now she didn't much care.

She could tell that Todd did, though. He had his nose mashed up against the screen, and he still hadn't taken his eyes off the lake.

"I haven't seen it yet," Jamie said. "But I haven't really been looking for it."

That made Todd turn around. "You haven't? Why not?"

Jamie shrugged and draped the towel around her neck. "It's been too cold to sit out here." She turned and headed out the screen door.

"Too cold?" Todd followed her down the steps. "Shoot. You should have told me. *I* would have come over and watched." He poked her in the arm and tried to give his southwestern twang a Dracula accent. "Don't forget, my dear. Ben Tyler perished in the cold. His ghost is most restless when it's shivering."

Jamie laughed. "Come on. Do you really still believe it?"

"I don't know. But I sure would like to find out whose light we saw all those times." Todd's dark brown eyes were sparkling, and Jamie knew he was hatching a plan to trap a "ghost."

Her mother was right. Todd was the schemer-dreamer, and it was usually Jamie who made the plans work. But this summer she wasn't interested in Tyler's ghost—not that she thought it existed. She was interested in a flesh-and-blood lifeguard. She didn't have any plan to get to know him, though, except by swimming a lot and looking as good as she could, but even if she had a plan, there was no way she could tell Todd about it. He wouldn't understand.

She kept quiet and listened with one ear while Todd talked on and on about how this was the summer they'd get to the bottom of the mysterious lantern and put the "ghost" to rest once and for all. By the time they got to the lake, she realized she hadn't said more than "uh-huh" a couple of times. Her mother would have called that rude, but Jamie knew Todd didn't mind. He probably hadn't even noticed, and that was the nice thing about being with him. She didn't have to explain herself.

When they got close to the water, Jamie started scanning the group of kids waiting to swim to the raft until she saw *him*.

He was standing with a clipboard in his hand, taking names. Instead of the red sweatshirt, he wore a red T-shirt and a yellow swimsuit—the uniform of the Sunrise Lake lifeguards. His back was to Jamie at first, but then he slowly turned around, looking to see how many more swimmers there were, and she saw the name stenciled on the front of his shirt. JIM. Jamie smiled to herself. She finally knew his name, and it was a little bit like hers. Maybe they were alike in other ways, too. All she wanted was a chance to find out.

"Come on," Todd said. "Let's get this over with so we can get some real swimming in before lunch."

They put their towels down and joined the crowd. Jeremy was already there with Todd's little brother. Both boys were dripping wet, and Jamie figured they'd already taken the test. She was glad. At least Jeremy wouldn't be bothering her. A little brother tagging along wouldn't help her image any.

When she saw Jim start toward them to take their names, Jamie stood up straight and gave a last tug to her swimsuit. How should she look? Should she stretch her legs so he'd think she was a superathlete? Should she smile at him or keep her eyes on the water so he wouldn't be able to tell how nervous she was? Would he remember her from the drugstore? If he did, would he say something?

21

"Todd Mitchell," Todd said to Jim.

Jamie took a deep breath. "Jamie Watson." She watched his hand scrawl her name on the pad of paper. She got a smile ready and moved her eyes up his tanned, muscular arm to his broad shoulder and finally to his face.

He didn't even glance at her. He was already moving on to the girl behind her. The nice smile was still on Jamie's face, but only Todd saw it.

"You look funny, Jamie."

"What do you mean, 'funny'?"

"I don't know. Sort of nervous." Todd nudged her with his elbow and laughed. "Afraid you won't make it to the raft?"

"Come on." Jamie decided to laugh, too, even though it was a little insulting to be told she looked "funny" when she was trying to look beautiful. "I'm a better swimmer than you are."

"You used to be." Todd grinned and pushed his sandy brown hair from his eyes. "This summer's going to be different."

"Hah." Jamie had to fight the urge to nudge him back. If she'd done that, though, they'd probably wind up in a towel-slapping fight, and that would really look juvenile. "You say that every summer."

"But this time I mean it. This summer I'm going the distance."

"Going the distance" meant swimming the width of Sunrise Lake at its widest point, which was a little over a mile. Neither Todd nor Jamie had ever tried it. It took a long time, and they'd always found more exciting things to do, like building bear rattles and hunting for snakes.

Jamie looked at him. "I suppose you want me to row alongside you in case you get a cramp?"

"I'm not going to get a cramp," Todd said. "I just want

you to row so you can cheer me on." He laughed and nudged her. "Then I'll do the same for you."

"Me? No, thanks. I don't want to spend hours in that water and come out shriveled like a raisin." They walked to the end of the pier together. "Not that I couldn't do it."

"Okay, next," Jim's voice called. "Mitchell?"

"Here," Todd said.

Jim checked his clipboard and nodded. "Go to it."

Jamie watched as Todd walked to the edge of the pier and dove in. She winced when she saw him land almost flat on his belly. He came up laughing and started swimming toward the rubber raft anchored about seventy-five feet out.

He really wasn't a very good swimmer, she thought. He splashed too much and tried to keep his head out of the water, which slowed him down and made him look clumsy. But style and grace didn't matter. All you had to do was prove you could swim.

Jamie glanced at Jim. He was yawning. Todd swam back, dripping and gasping, and waited with Jamie until it was her turn.

She dove in cleanly, surfaced, and pulled herself through the water with a smooth, strong stroke. She hoped Jim wasn't yawning, but even if he was, she knew he was finally looking at her. It was his job.

She reached the raft, caught her breath, and started back for the pier, using the backstroke this time. Todd reached over and helped her climb up onto the slippery boards. "Show-off," he said.

Jamie laughed and walked over to Jim to get the tag she'd have to wear every time she went swimming. It was a red decal that you stuck on your suit. Jamie was trying to decide where to put hers so that it would be visible but not too conspicuous. Then, suddenly, she felt Jim's fingers brush hers as he handed her the decal. She looked up to his face again, and this time his blue eyes were smiling right at *her* blue eyes.

"Jamie Watson?"

"Yes," Jamie said. "That's right."

"You look good in the water."

"Thank you." She tried to think of something else to say. Something clever. "I've always liked to swim." It wasn't clever, but it was better than nothing.

Jim laughed. "It's a good thing. I'm sure you didn't find any books to help you pass the time."

Jamie stared at him.

"That's where I saw you, wasn't it?" he asked. "In Spruce, at the drugstore? Looking through the book racks? The day before the deluge?"

Jamie nodded. This time she didn't even bother trying to think of anything to say. Just knowing that he remembered was enough.

"I thought so," he said. "Anyway, you ought to try for the distance this summer. Unless you've already done it."

"No. I haven't." Jamie was ready to swim ten miles if he wanted her to. "Maybe I'll give it a try."

He nodded. "Good."

"Hey, Jamie," Todd yelled. "Come on, let's do cannonballs off the pier."

Jamie looked at Jim, but he had already turned away, so she walked slowly over to Todd. She didn't want to do cannonballs. She wanted to stand next to Jim for the rest of her life.

☀ Three ☀

"What do you mean, you don't want to go hiking?"

"I mean I don't want to go hiking, that's all."

"But last night you said you'd come with me." Mrs. Watson sighed and frowned down at her new hiking boots. "Jamie, you don't seem to want to do anything with us this summer. Your father bought you those new hip boots just so you could do some stream fishing with him, and you haven't even worn them yet. You used to love hiking the trails with me, and now suddenly you don't want to go—again. The only place you go is the lake."

"I like the lake."

The Germ snickered. "She likes the lifeguard."

Jamie whirled around. "That's not true, so shut up!"

"Jamie!"

"I'm sorry. May I please go now?"

But Mrs. Watson was suddenly smiling. "Jamie, honey, is that it? Do you have a crush on some boy?"

"No!"

Jeremy snickered again, and Jamie wanted to pound him on the head. "I'm just—one of the lifeguards said I should do the mile swim this summer, that's all," she said. "Jeremy probably saw me talking to him and jumped to some juvenile conclusion." She took her towel and a thermos from the table. "I've been practicing so I can go the distance. You should be happy. You're always saying I never finish what I start."

Mrs. Watson stopped smiling and sighed again. "Well, it's your vacation, too, Jamie. Enjoy it the way you want to."

"I will. I mean, I *am* enjoying it." Jamie kissed her mother on the cheek. "See you later."

Jeremy followed her out onto the porch. "For somebody who's practicing, you sure spend a lot of time in the shallow water."

Jamie marched out the door without answering. What Jeremy said was true. She hadn't been swimming—actually swimming—very much. The day after the test, she'd decided to do some laps to the raft and back, but when she got there, Jim wasn't even on duty. She knew it was stupid, but she wanted him to see her, to know she was doing it for him. Why bother if he wasn't even there?

The next day, she tried again, but when she came out of the water, exhausted and shivering, he hadn't even looked at her. So then she just splashed around with Todd at the edge of the lake, but she couldn't really enjoy it. She was always wondering if Jim was watching.

The day before, though, she'd actually forgotten about him—for a while, anyway. Todd had found a bone in the water. It was about a foot long, knobby at one end and very sharp at the other. At first, they argued about whether

26

it was human or not, and when they couldn't decide, they started tossing it off the pier and diving for it. Jamie was having so much fun pretending to be a deep-sea diver that she didn't even hear the whistle until Todd punched her on the shoulder.

"We're in trouble," he said.

Jamie looked and saw Jim marching across the beach, onto the pier, and down to the end where she and Todd were standing. He was still beautiful, but his dimples didn't show because of his frown, and his blue eyes weren't smiling.

"Let me see that thing," he said, and his voice wasn't silky anymore.

Todd handed it to him. "It's a bone."

"That's obvious," Jim snapped. "It's also very jagged at one end, in case you hadn't noticed. The water here isn't all that deep, so unless you're looking for a gash in the head or a nice ugly cut in the eye, I suggest you find something less lethal to play with."

Jamie wanted to slip between the cracks in the pier and disappear from sight. Todd was blushing, and so was she; she could feel it. Jim hadn't even looked at her, but the way he talked made her feel about six years old, so she didn't really care.

He kept hold of the bone and started back to his chair. Then he stopped. "By the way, Jamie Watson," he said, "I haven't seen you make it to the other side of the lake yet." He grinned finally. "Don't disappoint me, okay?" He didn't wait for an answer; he just jogged down the pier on his long, lean legs.

Todd waited until he was far enough away. "Mr. Big Shot," he said in disgust.

"He was right," Jamie said.

27

"Who cares?" Todd pushed his hair out of his eyes and looked at her. "What did he mean about the other side of the lake?"

Jamie cleared her throat. "He told me I should try for it."

"He did?" Todd looked insulted. "He never said anything to me, and I was the one who was gonna shoot for it this summer, not you."

"Well, I'd like to try, too," Jamie announced. "Will you row for me?"

"Sure, I guess." Todd smiled. "Hey, Jamie, we'll be a team. You swim, and I'll be your trainer. Then you can do the same for me."

A few days later, Jamie was ready to go the distance. Or to try, anyway. She had a thermos of sweet tea for energy, and Todd was bringing his cassette recorder so she'd have something to listen to. She was going to swim across the lake, maybe even in record time, and prove to Jim that she wasn't a little kid. She would make him sit up and take notice!

Todd was waiting for her in the boat. He'd rowed over to the pier, just outside the rope that marked the swimming area. Jamie gave him her thermos and towel.

"Wait," she said. She unfolded the towel and took something out.

"What's that?"

"Haven't you ever seen a swimming cap before?" Jamie pulled it over her head and tucked up a few strands of hair. Her mother brought the cap every summer and used it for showering. "It'll cut down on friction," she said.

Todd laughed. "Jamie, for crying out loud! You act like you're swimming the English Channel. Why don't

28

you put grease all over your body? Maybe I should have brought an oxygen tank!"

Jamie ignored him and waded into the lake. It was only ten in the morning, and the water was icy. She shivered as it crept up her legs. She hated swimming in cold water.

She glanced back at the beach. Jim was in his chair. He hadn't seen her yet, but pretty soon he wouldn't be able to take his eyes off her—not if she could help it.

She kept going and gasped when the water lapped at her waist. Then she took a deep breath and dove forward. Behind her, she heard Todd splash the oars.

Her plan was to use the crawl until she got tired, then turn on her back and float for a minute or two until she got her breath, then go back to the crawl. Nothing fancy, just a clean, steady stroke.

She'd gone all of about fifteen yards when it happened. The right strap on her new swimsuit broke. She flipped onto her back. Two minutes later, the left strap went. She stopped and trod water.

"What's wrong?" Todd yelled. "Are you okay?"

"Uh." Jamie crossed her arms over her shoulders and stuck her chin up as far as she could. "Yeah. I just... I...it's—"

"You what? You what?" Todd had pulled the boat beside her. "Jamie?" He pulled the oars in and looked down.

Jamie saw his face go red. Todd was her best—her only—summertime friend, but she was too embarrassed to say a word. She took a deep breath and dipped beneath the water.

One of the straps had broken at the back and the other in the front. She thought she might be able to tie them together and somehow keep the suit up, but it was impossible. If she didn't drown, she'd wind up choking herself. She came up gasping. "Give me a hand. Please?"

29

Todd reached over, hauled her into the boat, and handed her a towel. Jamie arranged the towel around her so nothing showed. She was still too embarrassed to talk. She kept staring at her feet, feeling like an idiot. She hoped the Germ hadn't seen, or he'd tell her mother, and her mother would say, "I could have told you that suit was a big mistake."

For once, she even hoped that Jim hadn't been watching her, but this time she was out of luck. As she and Todd walked up the beach toward their cabins, Jim called down to her from his chair. "Hey, Jamie Watson, you're not giving up already, are you?"

"No." Jamie clutched the towel tighter and wished he'd stop using her last name.

"She just swallowed some water," Todd said. "She'll be back."

Jamie stared at him. He gave her an innocent smile. "Come on, Jamie. Let's ... uh ... let's discuss your strategy before you go back in."

Jim laughed. "Good idea. And don't forget about the undertow."

Jamie tried to smile and then walked on with Todd. Everybody knew a lake didn't have an undertow. Was Jim making fun of them? No, he couldn't be. He wasn't that kind of person; she was sure of it. He was probably just joking. He probably expected her to joke back. She should have said something like "I've been looking for that undertow for ages. If I find it, I'll tell you." Then he would have known she had a sense of humor, too. Now he probably thought she was just a dumb kid who couldn't get a joke *or* do the distance. Why couldn't she ever say the right thing at the right time? Even Todd was quicker— his lie about her swallowing water was so smooth she would have believed it herself if she hadn't known better.

30

She knew she ought to thank Todd, but she was feeling too humiliated to come right out and say, "Thanks for not mentioning my broken straps." She decided on another way to show her appreciation.

"Hey, Todd, I have an idea. I don't want to swim anymore today. Why don't we go exploring? Maybe to Tyler's cabin?"

"Great!" Todd's eyes lit up the way Jeremy's did when somebody mentioned ice cream. "I'll change and meet you in ten minutes." He took off running.

Jamie trudged back to her cabin, put on jeans and a bright blue tank top, and tied her yellow sweatshirt around her waist. She put the swimsuit in a plastic bag and stuffed it into a corner of her suitcase. As soon as it was out of sight, she felt much better.

By the time they reached Tyler's cabin, Jamie decided she was actually glad to be out of the water—and out of Jim's sight. Maybe she was being too obvious, spending so much time at the lake. Maybe if she stayed away once in a while, he'd notice. Besides, it was fun to hike through the woods with Todd, carrying a picnic lunch and pretending to be explorers, the way they used to. She didn't have to worry about her hair or her clothes or whether she was sweating a lot. Todd didn't care about those things, and when she was with him, she didn't, either.

Todd stopped ahead of her on the path and pulled a low-hanging pine branch aside. "There it is," he whispered, staring at the cabin.

"It looks just the same." Jamie was whispering, too, and she felt shivery inside.

Maybe it was because of the cabin. It wasn't fake old, like the ones at the lake. It was really old, and rotting, half-covered with vines and half-destroyed by weather.

It looked like an oversized, run-down outhouse, and Jamie could never imagine living in it—or dying in it.

She and Todd crept toward it as quickly as possible. It was a ritual with them even though it was daytime and they'd never found anyone there.

"The door's still on," Todd said. "Barely." He gave it a push, and they grinned at each other as it squeaked open.

The inside of the cabin was one of the things that kept the legend going. Its dirt floor was always packed hard and looked as though it had actually been swept; a few pieces of rusty tin cookware were stacked neatly in front of what used to be a fireplace; and an old, moth-eaten blanket was carefully folded in a corner.

It was always the same, from summer to summer. Two years before, Jamie and Todd had deliberately messed everything up, tossed the tin plates around, dug gouges in the floor with a stick, and had come back the next morning to find that somebody, or something, had cleaned up after them.

Todd touched her arm and pointed at the floor. "Footprints."

Jamie laughed. "Todd, those are ours."

"No, they're not." He put his feet in one set of prints and then the other. "See? They're both bigger than mine." He gave her a shove. "You stand in them."

The footprints weren't Jamie's, either.

"And look," Todd said. He pulled a piece of paper out of the blackened fireplace and spread it out.

Jamie looked and shivered. It was a Wonder Bread wrapper, obviously not from the eighteen hundreds.

"He's stealing food from the store in Spruce, I'll bet," Todd whispered. "Or from one of the lake cabins."

Suddenly, there was a loud banging at the door. Todd grabbed Jamie's hand, and the two of them stood close together, ready to face a ghost or a bear or whatever fate had in store.

Jamie was trying hard not to whimper when the door squeaked open and the Germ walked in, followed by Todd's brother, Dave.

"Gotcha!" Jeremy was laughing so hard he started to choke.

Dave grinned. "Bet you thought it was old Ben Tyler, huh?"

"You guys are so infantile." Jamie let go of Todd's hand and pounded Jeremy on the back. She really had been scared. "No, we didn't think it was the ghost."

"But look at this," Todd said. He showed them the bread wrapper. "We found it in the fireplace. It didn't get here on its own, did it?" He moved slowly toward Dave, shaking the wrapper and grinning like a maniac. "It's all that's left of the ghostly supper Ben Tyler ate last night. And tonight... he'll materialize again... in search of more food.... Maybe he'll even steal your Twinkies!"

"Who's being infantile now?" Dave didn't look scared at all. "There's no such thing as ghost."

"Then how did a Wonder Bread bag get in here?"

Jeremy smirked. "Lovers."

Jamie looked at him. "What are you talking about?"

"It's simple, stupid. Guys probably bring their girl-friends here all the time. They eat a little and smooch a lot."

At that point, Jamie's day was ruined all over again. As the four of them hiked back to the cabins, she munched a cheese sandwich and thought about Jeremy's theory. It was possible, she guessed, but she couldn't imagine going there with Jim. They'd have picnics, of course, and some beautiful day he'd kiss her, but not in some run-down shack. It might not have a ghost, but it was still a creepy place, as Todd said.

What made Jamie miserable, though, was the thought that Jim might have a girlfriend. He was so good-looking, she couldn't possibly be the only one who'd noticed. Of course, he was older; maybe even eighteen. He might like girls closer to his age. He might think of her as just another little girl he had to keep from drowning.

No, that couldn't be true. He'd singled her out that first day of swimming; he paid more attention to her than to any other girl on the beach, young or old. He'd even remembered their first meeting at the drugstore.

Jamie finished her sandwich and pulled on her sweatshirt. Maybe he was shy, like her, and didn't know how to express his feelings. Maybe she should tell him how she felt first. But how? What could she say? "Jim, I love you"?

Jamie almost laughed out loud. She'd never be able to say that, not at first, anyway. But that was what she felt, and she wanted to say it so badly she ached from keeping quiet.

That night, when everyone else was asleep, Jamie tried to say it in a letter to Carrie. She'd been at the lake almost two weeks and hadn't even sent her a postcard. She'd started a couple but never finished them.

Now she turned on her flashlight and fished a pad and pencil from her suitcase. She'd brought the paper because she wanted to write poetry, but after meeting Jim, she'd only written one: "Jim / Through the years / Our love will never / Dim." What a lousy poem. She should throw it in the fireplace and toast a marshmallow over it.

She crawled back into her sleeping bag, flipped the pad to a fresh sheet of paper, and rested the flashlight on her pillow so she could see to write.

Dear Carrie,

I'm sorry I haven't written, but I met the most won-
derful boy. His name is Jim, and he's a lifeguard here at
the lake. We . . .

Jamie stopped. We what? She and Jim hadn't done
anything. She crossed out "we" and started again.

He's so gorgeous you wouldn't believe it. I really like
him, and I think he likes me, too, because he told me I
should do the mile swim.

Jamie stopped again. She felt like crying. That's really
all Jim had done—suggest she swim across the lake. There
wasn't anything more to say except she loved him so
much it hurt, and she couldn't say that. She felt it, but
when she tried to put it into words, it sounded all wrong.
It just wasn't the kind of thing she could talk about or
write about. Maybe when something happened, she could
find the words. But for now she'd have to keep it to
herself, even though that hurt, too.

She turned off the flashlight, put the writing pad under
her pillow, and tried to sleep. Getting to sleep was becoming tricky. Every time she closed her eyes, she saw
Jim. Or her and Jim, walking by the lake in the moonlight,
holding hands. She was always wearing a soft, filmy dress,
and Jim was carrying her gold thin-strapped sandals. It
didn't matter that she didn't even own a soft, filmy dress
or that walking barefoot by a mountain lake at night was
a sure way to freeze your feet. In her imagination, nothing
seemed silly.

That night, though, Jamie couldn't keep the dream
going. She couldn't sleep, either, so she got out of bed,
then tiptoed through the kitchen and out onto the porch.
The icy air felt good at first. She leaned her head against
the screen and looked across the lake, wishing Jim were
standing beside her

That's when she saw it. The bobbing light. It was way, way off in the distance, but even so, Jamie could tell it was shining near the bend in Sunrise Lake, where Tyler's cabin was.

• *Four* •

"**G**eez, Jamie!" Todd was really insulted. "Why didn't you come get me?" he demanded the next morning when Jamie told him about the bobbing light.

Jamie cast her line into the stream where she and Todd were both fishing. "Todd, it was midnight. We couldn't have done anything, anyway."

"So what? At least I would have seen it!" he said in a loud whisper, trying not to scare away the fish.

Jamie reeled in and sloshed a little farther upstream. They were also fishing with her father and Mr. Mitchell, and Jamie was wearing her rubber hip boots for the first time. She hadn't wanted to—she could have fished from the bank—but she knew her father would have been disappointed, and she'd probably have gotten a lecture from her mother, so she'd put the dumb things on. They made her feel like a blimp. She was glad nobody else could see her, especially Jim.

She shook her head and threw her line in again. She was *not* going to think about him. There was no point in it. It was all just a dream. She was going to keep herself busy and keep Jim out of her mind, even if it meant sweating in ugly green hip boots.

"Hey, Todd," she called. "Next time I see the lantern, I'll come get you, okay?"

"Okay." Todd splashed upstream next to her. "But I don't want to just see it; I want to find out whose it is. Geez, Jamie, don't *you*?"

"Sure." Jamie really didn't, but at least it gave her something else to think about. "But we've got to have a plan."

"Yeah, I know. I think we should camp out next to the cabin. Then we'll be right on the spot when something happens."

Jamie shook her head. "Todd, we can't go camping out by ourselves. Nobody'd let us."

Todd started to protest. "Why? We're old enough to—" Then he turned red. "Oh, yeah, right," he said, and brushed the hair off his forehead.

Jamie noticed that his hair was getting bleached from the sun, like hers. It was also thick and curly, not like hers at all.

"Well," Todd said, a few moments later, "maybe my dad'll come with us. I could ask him."

"What are you going to say—that we want to catch Tyler's Ghost?" Jamie shook her head again. "No, we're just going to have to sneak out. That's the only way. The next time I see the lantern, we go."

Todd glanced downstream where Mr. Watson was helping Mr. Mitchell get his line unsnagged. "What if we get caught?"

"If we get caught, we get caught," Jamie said. "Let's worry about it if it happens. Now, do you want to do it or not?"

"Sure I do."

"Okay, then." Jamie was really getting into it now. She loved planning things. "I don't know when I'll see the lantern, so we have to be prepared."

"Right," Todd said. "How?"

"We'll keep our duffel bags ready so we don't have to crash around in the middle of the night looking for things and wake everybody up." She thought a second. "Put a jacket in it and socks—warm stuff. And a flashlight. I'll keep a box of crackers or something in mine."

"For the ghost?"

"Are you kidding? For us!" Jamie laughed and gave him a push. Todd laughed, too, and pushed her back. She took an off-balance step, and her foot came down on a smooth, slippery rock. She threw out her hand and grabbed the first thing available, which was Todd's arm, but he was as off-balance as she was. In a second, they were both sitting in the stream, feeling the icy mountain water seep into their boots.

Jamie tried to struggle to her feet, but she was laughing too hard. Todd took their poles and heaved them onto the bank, and for a few seconds they just sat side by side in the water, giggling.

They were still laughing when the four of them trudged back to the cabins a short time later. Their fathers were grumbling about having their fishing time cut short, but Jamie knew they weren't really that upset. They'd caught a few fish, and they could play cards the rest of the afternoon until it was time for the cookout the two families were having on the beach that evening.

Jamie was actually looking forward to the cookout. Two days earlier, she would have tried to figure a way

39

to get out of it, but after joking with Todd and planning the ghost hunt, she felt better than she had since she'd come to the lake. It was always fun to be out on the beach at night when most everybody else was gone, sitting around a fire and telling stories or singing.

They were walking along a path just above the beach when she saw Jim. Or rather, she saw his feet and his head. The rest of him was surrounded—by girls. Most of them were younger than Jamie was, but that didn't matter. They were with him; some of them were close enough to touch him, and one was even holding his hand.

Jim must have just gotten off duty and was tossing a Frisbee with them. As Jamie watched, he threw the Frisbee; a girl caught it on one finger, and Jim congratulated her with a big hug. Jamie hated that girl, even though she only looked about ten years old. She also hated herself for feeling that way, but she couldn't help it. She wanted to be the only one romping on the beach with him, the only one he saw, the only one he touched. Instead, she was trudging along, dripping wet, a pair of huge hip boots in one hand and a bunch of dead fish dangling from the other.

"Hey, Jamie," Todd said. "Maybe you'll see the lantern again tonight. Wouldn't that be great?" Todd was soaked, too, but he seemed totally unaware of it. His eyes were bright, and he kept pushing at his hair, the way he did when he was excited. "I bet we're the ones who finally find out what it's all about."

"Hey, Jamie, watch it," her father said. "That's part of our dinner lying there at your feet."

Jamie took her eyes off Jim long enough to notice that she'd dropped the fish, which were now covered with dirt and pebbles.

As she bent to pick the disgusting things up, Todd said, "We're probably going to be famous around here. Years from now they'll still be talking about Mitchell and Watson, the ones who solved the riddle of Tyler's Ghost." He laughed and switched his boots to his other shoulder, sprinkling Jamie with water.

"I'm not interested in being famous," Jamie snapped. "At least not for doing some dumb thing like going after a ghost that doesn't even exist."

Todd's mouth fell open, like one of the fish's. Then he took a deep breath. "But Jamie. Hey, I thought—"

Jamie didn't wait to hear what he thought. She marched off without looking back. She didn't want to be on the beach a minute longer. She wanted to get away from Todd and his schemes. She wanted to get away from the sight of Jim, surrounded by silly little girls. She wanted to disappear, but she didn't have anyplace to go but her cabin.

In her room, she drew the blanket across the door, pulled off her wet clothes, crawled into her sleeping bag, and slept until dinnertime.

"Jamie, you've hardly touched your food." Alice Mitchell was a thin woman with a big appetite who thought everybody else could eat as much as she did. "I've been watching you, honey. All you've done is pick, pick, pick, just like a bird."

"Well, birds eat a lot for their size, Mrs. Mitchell." Jamie saw her mother raise an eyebrow. "And I've already had two helpings of your potato salad," she said quickly. "It's really good."

"That recipe's been in my family for ages," Mrs. Mitchell said. "The trick is to mash the egg yolk before you add it to the potatoes."

"Oh. Well, it's really good," Jamie said again. "I think I'll have some more." She wasn't really interested in the secrets of the Mitchell family potato salad, so she excused herself to get another helping that she didn't want.

41

She plopped some more salad onto her plate and moved to the other side of the campfire. Nobody was sitting there, because the wind was blowing that way, but Jamie wanted to be alone, so she tried to ignore the smoke that kept wafting into her eyes and down her throat.

They'd been on the beach for two hours, and it was almost dark enough to see the stars. All that was left of the cookout were a bunch of fish bones, some gnawed ears of corn, and some of the famous potato salad. It was almost time for charred marshmallows and off-key singing.

"So when she told me Todd and Jamie were both missing, I knew they had to be together." Mr. Mitchell laughed. "And where did I find them? About sixty yards away. Todd had persuaded Jamie to go snake hunting and gotten them lost. But Jamie was heading in the right direction when I found them, even though they were only about five at the time."

"Jamie always could find her way back," Mr. Watson said. He peered across the campfire. "How you doing over there, Jamie? You choking yet?"

Jamie forked up another bite of salad and tried not to cough. "I'm fine, Dad."

"Hurry up and eat," her mother called. "Dan's about ready to get out his guitar. You and Todd can serenade us."

"Oh, yes," Mrs. Mitchell said. "I want to hear 'My Darling Clementine.' You two haven't sung for us this entire vacation." She turned to Jamie's mother. "Remember the first time they sang together? They forgot the words and started crying and woke up the babies."

Jamie kept on chewing while everybody else laughed. She and Todd were famous for their duets, but she had a feeling they wouldn't be singing together that night. Todd was sitting between Jeremy and Dave. He hadn't moved all evening. He'd eaten and talked a lot, but he'd also stared at the ground a lot. Jamie knew him well enough to realize that meant he was upset. She also knew why. He was upset with *her* because of the way she'd acted on the beach that afternoon. She'd gotten him all excited about finding the ghost, then made him feel like a kid for getting caught up in her plans. She kept telling herself to apologize, but she knew that if she did, she'd probably start crying—not about the way she'd acted but about Jim.

She pushed the food around on her plate, trying to make it look as though she'd eaten most of it. It didn't work. Mr. Mitchell hauled out his guitar from its battered case and started strumming. He was a little rusty, but ordinarily that wouldn't have mattered to Jamie. Music usually cheered her up. That night, even music didn't help.

"Come on, Jamie, Todd," Mrs. Mitchell said. "Let's hear 'Clementine.'"

Jamie stood up and coughed. She didn't have to pretend; the smoke made her throat feel like sandpaper. "I don't think I can," she said. "Sorry. I feel like maybe I'm catching a cold."

"No wonder," Jeremy said. "Daddy told us how you fell into the stream and then sat there for ten minutes without even trying to get up."

Everybody else laughed, but suddenly Jamie was furious. "You try getting up when your hip boots are full of water. I'd like to see it. You'd probably drown."

"Jamie," her mother said, "nobody's laughing at you. We're laughing at the situation. Why are you so touchy?"

"I'm not touchy. I'm just tired of the Germ bugging me all the time. Why don't you tell him to stop?"

"I'll stop when you stop calling me Germ," Jeremy shouted. "I hate it! Anyway, I'm not bugging anybody. You are. Why don't you just buzz off?"

Everyone was too surprised to say anything for a minute, but Jamie could tell her mother wouldn't take long to get started, so she decided to follow the Germ's advice.

She knew that the worst thing about walking off in a huff was when nobody came after you and you had to keep going even if you didn't have anyplace to go. No one came after her this time, so she kept going.

She walked until she came to the pier. It was dark out there over the water, and she was trying to think of a way to apologize gracefully and get herself off the hook when she noticed the figure standing at the very end of the pier. Even in the dark, she could tell it was Jim. He was standing exactly the way she'd seen him on that first day at the lake—his hands on his hips, his feet slightly apart, staring out at the water.

Jamie wasn't sure what to do. There they were, alone on the beach, just the way she'd imagined. Of course, she had on an orange sweatshirt and faded jeans rolled to the knees instead of a dress, and Jim wasn't carrying her gold-strapped sandals, but everything else was the same. All she had to do was put one foot in front of the other and walk out to him.

She glanced back toward the campfire. Everyone was still there; she could see their shadows and hear them singing.

She turned back to the pier. If she didn't do something then, she never would. She took one step and fell flat on her face.

He turned around immediately. "Who is it? Are you okay?"

"Uh-huh." Jamie struggled to her knees. By the time he got to her, she was transferring the slimy grime from her hands to her jeans. "I—my sneaker got caught in one of the cracks."

"Well, hi, Jamie Watson." Jim bent down, took her hand, and helped her to her feet. He was smiling. "Are you wandering around out here all by yourself?"

"No, I'm with them." She pointed to the campfire. "I just felt like being alone."

"Umm, I know what you mean." He let go of her hand. "That's why I took a stroll, too."

She wasn't sure whether to stay or go. If he wanted to be alone, maybe she'd better let him. He already was moving back toward the water. She stayed where she was.

He stopped. "Well, come on. There's room for two," he said, helping her steady herself.

Side by side, they walked out to the end of the pier. Jamie felt shivery, but she knew it wasn't from the cold. She could still feel the pressure of his hand on hers when he pulled her up from the ground. The moon was out, and she could see its path on the lake. They stood together a couple of minutes while she fretted about what to say, but Jim didn't seem to care whether she said anything at all. He was looking at the stars, so she did, too.

Finally, he said, "There's a falling star."

Jamie nodded. "Did you wish on it?"

"Sure I did." He laughed, and his voice was even more beautiful in the dark. "Did you?"

"Yes." Jamie wasn't about to tell him what she'd wished for, and, luckily, he didn't ask. She wanted to hear him talk again though, so she blurted out, "I saw the northern lights once."

"You're kidding. Where? I thought you could only see them up in the Arctic."

"No. This was in Montana. My parents took us camping there once when I was real young." She hoped he wouldn't ask how old she was now. If he found out she was only fourteen, he might not want anything to do with her.

But he just kept staring at the sky. "You must be a real nature girl."

She didn't know whether to admit it or deny it. She only wanted to give the answer that would please him. "Well, sort of. I like the water, anyway." Hadn't she already told him that?

"You already told me that." He laughed and bent his head close to hers. Then he whispered, "But I still haven't seen you go the distance."

❋ Five ❋

"Do you believe this day, Mom?" Jamie broke away from her mother and strode ahead on the narrow trail. She threw her arms above her head and laughed up at the sky. "Look at it!"

"Jamie." Mrs. Watson stopped and wiped her forehead. "You've been going like you're on the way to a fire since we started out. Slow down a little, why don't you?"

Jamie waited until her mother caught up to her. "I don't get it. One minute you're griping that I won't come hiking with you. Then when I finally do, you gripe about that."

"I'm not griping." Mrs. Watson rubbed her legs. "I'm delighted that we're out together, even if it is only eight o'clock in the morning."

"I couldn't sleep another minute. Anyway, this is the best time; you always said so."

"I know, I know. Believe me, I admire your energy, Jamie. I'm just asking you to remember that I'm not fourteen anymore."

"Okay." Jamie looked up the trail. Now that she'd stopped, she realized she was getting hungry. "Let's just go a little bit farther, till we get to the top of the bluff. We can eat breakfast there."

"Breakfast? All I want is a massage and a nap."

Jamie laughed again and started climbing. They'd been out for over an hour; she'd been awake since six o'clock and still hadn't eaten, but she felt terrific, as if she owned the mountain.

From the top of the bluff they could see valleys and mountains that seemed to stretch forever. They admired the view and then sat down to eat the sandwiches Jamie had brought. After they ate, her mother groaned and closed her eyes, so Jamie pulled out a pad and pencil and started her third letter to Carrie.

Last night was so beautiful, I'm not sure I can describe it. I met this boy—a lifeguard who works here at the lake—and last night, we talked, really talked, for the first time.

Mrs. Watson shifted around. Without opening her eyes, she said, "What are you writing?"

"A letter."

"Oh."

Last night, I bumped into him on the pier. He was all alone, and so was I. Actually, I'd just had a big fight with the Germ on the beach, and everybody was mad at me, so I left.

"Who?"

Jamie looked over at her mother. "Who what?"

"Whom are you writing?"

"Carrie."

"Oh, that's nice. She's already written you, hasn't she?"

"Umm."

Did I tell you his name's Jim? And that he's gorgeous? Well, he is. No, he's beautiful. He has blond hair and blue eyes and dimples, and you'd think he'd have about fifteen girlfriends. But last night, when we were alone— together—I got the feeling that he was lonely and that maybe he liked being with me.

"What are you writing her?"

"Just stuff."

"Stuff? What kind of letter is that?"

"Mother. It's private, for crying out loud." Jamie tossed her pencil down, and before she could stop it, it rolled over the edge of the bluff. She waited until it stopped clattering on the rocks below. "Now look what happened."

Mrs. Watson pushed her hat back from her eyes. "I trust you're not blaming me for that."

Jamie started to frown but then changed her mind and laughed instead. She was feeling too good to let anything spoil her mood.

Her mother laughed, too. "I'm sorry, honey. I didn't mean to pry. I was just curious, I guess. You seem so much happier this morning than you were last night, I thought you might be telling Carrie the reason and maybe you'd tell me. You know, we were a little worried about you when you went storming off last night. Where did you go?"

"Just for a walk on the pier, like I said before." Jamie looked back down at the letter. She knew it would make her mother happy if she shared it with her, but she couldn't.

After she and Jim had had the conversation about her being a "nature girl," they'd turned around to walk back to the shore. That's when she'd noticed that her family and the Mitchells were packing up, and she realized she'd stayed away too long.

"Uh-oh, I've got to go, Jim," she'd said regretfully.

"Good night, Jamie Watson," he'd called after her. "See you on the beach."

She hadn't said anything about Jim when she got back to the campfire, and she still didn't want to tell her mother about meeting him. There was no way she could talk about Jim without sounding like the girls who giggled over some cute boy in the halls at school. She could still feel Jim's hand on hers and his breath on her ear, but she knew if she said so, it would sound ridiculous. Even her letter to Carrie was all wrong.

"Mom," she said, "there's nothing to tell, really. I'm just feeling good." She stood up. "In fact, I'm feeling so good, I think I'll swim across the lake."

This time, Jamie wasn't taking any chances. Her old black tank suit was hardly sexy, but its inch-wide straps couldn't possibly break, because the whole suit was all one piece of material. She didn't bother to try to see her two halves in the bathroom mirror, either. She knew exactly how she looked in that old swimsuit, but that day it didn't matter. She felt beautiful—because of Jim—and that's what counted. Besides, if she gave herself a really critical once-over, she might forget the feeling and start counting the flaws.

She filled a thermos with juice, grabbed a couple of big soft towels, and then found Todd just as he was leaving his cabin.

"Hi, Todd."

"Oh, hi."

"You busy?"

"Not really." He shrugged. "I was just going to go into Spruce, see if maybe the drugstore has any magazines less than two months old." He left his porch, and Jamie fell into step beside him.

"They won't," she said. "My mother was there yesterday to get a newspaper, and she said the magazine racks are empty."

"Oh." Todd shrugged again. "Well, maybe I'll get a newspaper instead. I didn't bring any books."

"But what do you want to read for? This is a great day. Don't you want to swim or something?"

Todd stopped on the path and picked up a rock. "Not really. I'm getting a little bored with swimming."

"Bored?"

"Oh, you know." Todd tossed the rock toward the lake and missed it by about thirty yards. "After about three weeks at this place, you start to look for other things to do." He tossed another rock.

Jamie looked at him. His sandy hair hung over his forehead, and he hadn't even bothered to push it back, so he must really be bored. She'd never seen Todd bored before. He was usually excited about some plan or other.

Then she remembered. Tyler's Ghost. She'd told Todd she didn't want to have anything to do with it after she'd promised him she would and they'd already started making plans. She must have really hurt his feelings, but she'd been flying so high since talking to Jim the night before that she hadn't even thought about anything else, least of all Tyler's Ghost.

She still wasn't interested in going after it, but maybe if she agreed to do it, she could talk Todd into rowing the boat for her. After all, she *had* promised him.

"Listen, Todd. I was thinking of going into Spruce, too, for some, uh, rope."

"What do you want rope for?"

Jamie thought fast. "Who knows what we'll find when we go after the lantern? Personally, I don't think it'll be a ghost, but—I don't know—we might need to tie somebody up."

51

"That's crazy." Todd took a handful of rocks. "I didn't want to capture anybody. I just wanted to see." One by one, he threw the rocks. "Anyway, let's forget about it."

"What do you mean?" Jamie scooped up a handful and started tossing, too.

"Oh, it was a dumb idea."

"It was not."

"It was too. You said so yourself yesterday."

They were close to the lake now, and Jamie watched as Todd sent one of his rocks skipping over the surface. Then she said, "But that was yesterday. Anyway, it's not a bad idea. It's just an idea whose time hasn't come yet, that's all." *Poor Todd*, she thought. *If only he knew why I keep changing my mind.* But Todd was the last person Jamie wanted to tell about Jim.

"Well, I'm ready for one whose time *has* come," he said. His next rock skipped three times before it sank, and he grinned. "Think you can beat that?"

"Sure." Jamie grinned back. "And if I do, will you row for me while I swim the distance?"

Todd looked surprised. "I thought you'd given up on that."

"I did, for a while. But now I'm ready to try again." She thought of Jim and tried not to blush. "I feel like a winner today."

"Today?"

"Sure, right now," Jamie said. "Right after I win this rock-skipping contest."

Todd shook his head and laughed. "Okay. It's a deal. And after you go the distance, we'll go into Spruce for that rope. Now, remember to use a smooth, flat rock. They work best."

"I know, I know." Jamie searched the ground until she found one.

"Now, don't forget, you've got to flick your wrist. It's all in the wrist, Jamie." He pushed at his hair and demonstrated.

"You're trying to psych me out, right?"

"Of course not. There isn't any contest." Todd examined the rock she'd picked. "Not bad. A little on the rough side. A four-skipper maybe, never a five."

"Five?" Jamie laughed. "Oh, no, you challenged me to beat a three."

"Oh, right. I forgot. Sorry." Casually, Todd skimmed another rock over the water.

"Show-off." Jamie was really into the game now.

"Are you kidding? I'm giving you pointers, that's all."

"Just give me some room." Jamie took a position and slid the rock between her thumb and forefinger. She drew back her arm and threw, remembering to flick her wrist. The rock landed with a plop and sank immediately.

She looked back to where Todd had been standing. But he wasn't there any longer. He was already heading for the rowboat.

"How you doing, Jamie?"

"Okay." Jamie spit some water out of her mouth and squinted up at the sky. "How far have I gone?"

"Don't think about that yet; you'll just get discouraged. You want some juice?"

"Not yet," Jamie said, as she floated for a while on her back. She had already gone about half the distance.

"Okay," Todd said. "Let me know."

"I will." Jamie flipped back onto her stomach. She might not be able to skip stones, but she could swim, and as she'd told Todd, she felt like a winner that day.

While she swam, images of Jim kept flashing through her mind—Jim sitting in his lifeguard chair, striding along the beach in the rain, and especially, standing at the end of the pier, staring up at the stars.

She knew Jim was on the beach, but she hadn't even told him what she was doing. She'd decided to just do it and then surprise him.

She was imagining the scene. She'd walk up from the lake, tired but smiling, and say, "I just went the distance." And he'd look down at her and smile back, and he'd say . . .

"Jamie! Get out of the water! Now!"

It wasn't Jim, of course. It was Todd, and he sounded scared. Jamie stopped swimming and started treading, but before she could ask what was wrong, a wave swamped her and almost rolled her completely over. By the time she broke the surface, a second wave hit her.

She came up sputtering and saw Todd sitting in the rowboat, which was heaving and bucking as if it were on the high seas during a storm.

Then she heard the noise—sort of a cross between a buzz saw and a toy airplane with a whining motor. "A speedboat? What's it doing here? It's supposed to be at the other end of the lake."

"*Two* speedboats, and never mind where they're supposed to be," Todd yelled. "They're here, so get in the boat before you drown."

He reached out both hands and pulled her up beside him. "Here they come again. Hang on!"

Jamie watched as the two speedboats raced around just outside the swimming area. They were beautiful, sleek as sharks, and if they hadn't been heading right at her and Todd, she might have enjoyed the sight. As it was, she closed her eyes and held on to the boat.

Then she decided she'd rather see the end of her life approaching, so she opened her eyes again. The two boats came closer, side by side, then split apart, as if the little

54

rowboat were a rock they didn't want to graze their hulls on.

Jamie caught a glimpse of one of the drivers as he roared by. He didn't glance her way, just raised one hand in the air and waved casually. She tightened her grip on the sides of the boat while it rocked back and forth and tried to keep her stomach from rocking with it. When the speedboats looked like specks of silver and sounded like mosquitoes, Jamie finally let her breath out.

☀ *Six* ☀

A big crowd was waiting for them on shore, and when Jamie climbed out of the rowboat, the first face she saw was Jim's. He was angry, but when he put his hand on her shoulder, she knew he wasn't angry at *her*.

"Are you two okay?"

Jamie nodded and hoped he'd never take his hand away.

"We're okay now," Todd answered. "But it was a little scary."

"I'll bet." Jim bent down and peered into Jamie's face. "Are you sure you're all right, Jamie Watson? You look a little green around the gills, as my mother would say."

"My mother says that, too." Jamie smiled at him. She'd been terrified, but now that it was over, with Jim touching her and looking so worried, she knew she wouldn't have missed it for the world. "But I'm fine, really. I just never expected to see speedboats out there."

"Nobody did." Bob, one of the other lifeguards, looked mad enough to spit. "Those jerks. They could have killed somebody. Or themselves. Did you get a good look at the boats?"

"Not really," Todd said. "One was kind of silvery, but I don't know about the other one."

"It was orange," Jamie said. "With a lot of chrome. The driver was young." She looked at Jim. "Maybe your age. He had blond hair, like yours, and he waved at me when he went by."

"Jerk," Bob said again. "Do you think you could identify him?"

"No." Jamie wanted to be helpful, but she knew she'd never recognize the guy again. "He was going too fast."

"That's okay." Jim took his hand off Jamie's shoulder and smiled. "I think I can find them. There aren't that many speedboats up at the other end of the lake." He turned to Bob. "You don't mind taking over a little early, do you?"

Bob shook his head. "When you find them, tell them they nearly drowned a little girl."

Jamie cringed at the words, but Jim laughed. "Little girl? She was going for the distance." He looked at Jamie. "I was watching you, Jamie Watson. You were doing okay. Don't give up." He touched her shoulder again and then went off to find the owners of the speedboats. Bob walked to the lifeguard chair, and after asking some questions and speculating on what the boats were doing out of bounds, the rest of the crowd went back to what they'd been doing before the big excitement.

"Jamie?"

"Huh?"

"You sure you're okay?" Todd looked worried. "Maybe you ought to go back to the cabin and take a rest or something."

57

Jamie finally took her eyes off Jim's disappearing figure. "I'm fine, Todd," she said. "I've never felt better in my life."

At first, she and Todd hung around the beach, waiting for Jim to come back and tell them he'd found the culprits, but after an hour or so, Todd started to get restless. "They were probably new at the lake and didn't know the boundaries," he said. "We're all right, so who cares? Even if he finds them, he's not exactly going to haul them back for a trial." He picked up a rock, skimmed it over the water, and grinned at her. "Hey, what about our deal, Jamie? Let's go into Spruce and find some rope."

"Sure, let's go," Jamie said.

They didn't find any rope in Spruce, at least not any they could afford, but they did find food. Jamie was suddenly starving to death, and the smell from Taylor's lunch counter was irresistible. She hadn't had a cheeseburger or a chocolate shake since she'd left home, and they were perfect for her terrific mood. Todd wolfed down two of the greasy burgers, so he must have felt the same way, even though Jamie figured it had to be for a different reason. After all, Todd wasn't in love.

Every time she remembered Jim's hand on her shoulder and the worried look in his eyes, Jamie felt like smiling. She carried that feeling with her through the rest of the day, and when she went to bed, she didn't have to conjure up any impossible images of the two of them on the beach together. What had happened that afternoon was better than anything she could have dreamed up. She was glad she and Todd got back to their cabins, glad to be alone, so she could think about Jim all by herself.

She wasn't sure what she was dreaming about when she heard the noise. Probably about Jim. Jamie knew people smiled in their sleep, and she was sure she must have had a mile-wide grin on her face when a clanking, rattling crash made her sit straight up in bed.

She heard a lot of rustling just outside the cabin, and at first she was frightened. Then Jeremy gave a shout of excitement, her parents started to make familiar grumbling noises, and Jamie finally realized that her brother had resurrected the bear rattle.

She was laughing when she joined Jeremy outside. "Well, was it a bear?"

"I don't know." Jeremy aimed his flashlight at the overturned garbage can. "I didn't get here fast enough to see." He pointed to several paw prints in the dirt. "What do you think?"

"I'm not sure," Jamie said. "They're definitely not raccoon, but they look kind of small for a bear."

"So maybe it was a small bear. Or a cub." Jeremy looked hopeful, and Jamie didn't feel like arguing, so she said, "Maybe it was, Jer."

They both jumped when their father's voice bellowed from the porch, "Well, if it *was* a bear, you two are sitting ducks. Clean that garbage up and get inside. And don't bring that can with you. Bury it!"

Jeremy suddenly looked very pale and frightened, and Jamie tried hard not to laugh again. "Don't worry, Jer," she said. "Whatever it was, it's long gone. If the bear rattle didn't scare it off, Daddy's voice did."

Jeremy shivered and Jamie knew he wasn't convinced. "Go ahead and get inside," she said. "I'll clean up."

"Okay." He was up the steps and onto the porch in about two seconds. "Thanks, Jamie."

Left alone, Jamie didn't feel quite so brave. The flashlight only made the dark seem darker, and the wind made a very animal-like rustling in the trees. She stuffed the garbage back in the can, grabbed the rattle, which she decided to stow away somewhere until her father had forgotten about it, and ran inside as fast as possible.

Safe on the other side of the sagging screen door, Jamie realized she was wide awake. She could hear her mother snoring and knew her father must be asleep, too, or he would have been griping about it while he tried to get her to turn over. Jeremy didn't snore exactly, but he did sleep with his mouth open and always made a lot of munching, smacking sounds. She could hear him now and knew he was asleep, too.

It was cold on the porch, and she was trying to decide whether to snuggle into her sleeping bag and relive the day's events or start another letter to Carrie when she saw the lantern off in the distance, bobbing and dipping through the trees at the bend in the lake.

Jamie almost giggled. She wasn't sure why, but she couldn't wait to tell Todd. Maybe it was because she was feeling good enough to try anything, or maybe the bear rattle had made her remember how much fun they used to have, sneaking out together at night, waiting for bears, and scaring themselves silly. She decided to follow the feeling, no matter what its reason was.

In five minutes, she dressed, took her ready-packed duffel bag, and tiptoed past the open-mouthed Jeremy and then out the screen door. She'd forgotten her flashlight, but she knew the path between her cabin and the Mitchells' so well she could have walked it with her eyes closed. It was a good thing, too, since it was so dark her eyes might as well have been closed.

Todd had the same room in his cabin as she did in hers. She knelt down beneath his window, scooped up a handful of small pebbles, and tossed a couple of them at the screen. Silence.

She waited until the wind picked up a little and then tossed a few more. Still no response. She tried a "Psst!" and then tried it again, a little louder.

Finally, Todd's face peered out the window. He looked pale and puffy from sleep. He yawned, then whispered, "What's up?"

"The lantern," Jamie whispered back. "I saw it. Just now. Got your stuff?"

Todd nodded, and his head disappeared. Jamie waited in the dark for about two minutes—not quite long enough for her to get totally terrified—and then Todd was beside her, gear in hand, eyes wide open. "You really saw it?"

"I wouldn't be out here if I didn't," Jamie said. "Come on, let's take one of the boats across the lake."

"Why a boat? Why the lake? Geez, Jamie, that doesn't make any sense."

"Jeremy put the bear rattle out tonight, and something knocked it off." Jamie was moving along the path as fast as she could without tripping and making a racket. "I don't want to take any chances. If there's a bear around, we'll be safe on the water."

Todd almost snorted. "Sure, but we'll have to get out of the boat and walk to the cabin, you know." He switched to his Dracula voice. "Don't forget, my dear, the bear is a cunning animal. No doubt it will be waiting for us on the other side of the lake, claws and fangs at the ready!"

"Ssh!" Jamie shivered, part in fear, part in excitement. "Don't try to be logical. Just try to be quiet."

When they got to the boat, they threw their bags in and, with a lot of shushing and splashing, pushed it into the water and climbed in.

Jamie rowed first, but she couldn't keep from slapping the oars, so Todd took over, although he wasn't that much quieter. Once they were out of the trees and under the open sky, the moon gave them some light, but not enough as far as Jamie was concerned. She couldn't quite believe what she was doing, but for some reason, she couldn't stop. She wasn't scared exactly, but it was so quiet she wanted to shout.

61

"Hey, Jamie," Todd said suddenly, "what classes are you taking next year?"

"I'm not sure. The guidance counselor told me most of the courses I had to take. The only thing I really got to pick for myself was French."

"Oh. Are you excited about it?"

"About French?"

"No, about high school."

"I guess so," Jamie said. "I guess I'm a little nervous, too."

"I know what you mean. High school's a lot more important."

"It is?"

"Sure. From there it's college, and from *there* it's real life. That makes me nervous."

"Oh." Jamie had been thinking about the social pressures, not the academic ones. "Well, do you get good grades?"

"So-so." Todd was finally rowing steadily and quietly. A slight wind rocked the boat from time to time, but not enough to make them want to abandon ship. "What about you?"

"I do okay," Jamie said. "When I try."

Todd laughed. "My problem is, I always get sidetracked. It seems like there's always something I'd rather be doing. Not just hanging out, I mean, but another book I'd rather read, or . . . I don't know. Anyway, I just hope I can keep my mind on high school."

Jamie remembered something. "Once when I didn't want to do my homework—I was about eight—my mother said, 'If you do it and keep doing it, you'll only have to go to school for twelve years to get a high school diploma. If you don't do it, who knows how long it'll take?' That kept me going for a long time."

"It makes sense, at least." Todd laughed again. "But I want to go to college, too, so I've got that to think about." He dipped the oars into the water without making a sound, and then he sighed. "And then there's girls."

Jamie sat up straighter. "Girls?"

"Sure. You know, dating and stuff. That's a whole new ball game that I don't even know how to play."

Jamie knew exactly what he was talking about, but she was surprised to find out that Todd was such a worrier or that they even worried about the same things. She also never thought she'd be having such a conversation in the middle of the night in the middle of a lake. It was strange, but at least it took her mind off things like drowning and bears and ghosts. "I know what you mean," she said. "Except *I* worry about boys."

They laughed together, and then Todd rested the oars and glanced back at her. "We're almost at the other side. You sure you want to go through with this?"

Jamie took a deep breath and nodded. "I just hope we find something, that's all."

"We will. You'll see." Todd grinned and rowed as close to the shore as he could. They both leaped onto the bank and dragged the boat up as far as they could so it wouldn't slide back into the lake. They picked up their bags, looked at each other, and then Jamie said, "Let's go."

They'd walked about ten feet into the woods when Jamie heard the alarm siren. She'd heard it before, not very often, but often enough to know what it meant. It meant a boat had been discovered missing, and the crew was going to search the lake to make sure no one had drowned. It meant floodlights and an official motorboat and worried families. She also knew that this time it meant that somebody had found out that she and Todd were gone.

She looked at Todd, and for a minute she was afraid he was going to cry. "We have to go back," she said. She didn't want to say it, but it was obvious that if she didn't, he'd keep marching right into the woods. "We can't let them look for us all night."

Todd didn't cry; he just stared up the path he'd wanted to take for a long, long time. Then he sighed, and finally he nodded. They went back to the boat and pushed it into the water. Jamie rowed. It didn't matter how much noise she made now.

The crew met them in the middle of the lake and escorted them the rest of the way back. Jamie and Todd kept quiet the whole time, except when Todd, who seemed to have recovered, said, "Boy, are we in *big* trouble," and Jamie laughed hysterically. She stopped immediately when Bob the lifeguard gave her a dirty look.

The crowd waiting on the shore was hardly as friendly as the one that had greeted them that afternoon. It wasn't even a crowd, really, just the two families and a couple of men from the crew. But to Jamie it seemed like thousands, with every one of them ready to yell at her.

As she got out of the boat, she quickly scanned the group, which was dressed in a strange assortment of pajamas and hiking clothes, trying to find Jim. When she saw him, she couldn't read the expression on his face. He wasn't smiling, but he didn't look furious, either. Maybe he was just sleepy. Whatever he was, Jamie couldn't face him. She stared at her feet for as long as she could and then finally lifted her eyes and faced her parents.

☀ Seven ☀

"Do you have any idea how worried we were?" Mr.
Watson demanded as he paced back and forth in front of
the fireplace. He was still wearing his down vest over a
pair of blue-and-white striped pajamas, and if he hadn't
been so angry, Jamie would have laughed at the sight.
"Do you realize what a thoughtless, reckless, dangerous—"

"Juvenile," Jeremy put in.

"Right, 'juvenile' thing that was to do?"

"I'm sorry, Dad." Jamie shifted around on the floor
and sneaked a peek at Todd. It was almost two o'clock
in the morning, and both families were gathered in the
Watsons' cabin. The adults were taking turns lecturing.

"I'm really sorry," Jamie said again.

"We believe you are, Jamie," Mrs. Mitchell said softly.
She looked more sad than angry. "What we want to know
is why you did it."

65

"Yes," Jamie's mother said. She was wrapped in a blanket and didn't look sad at all. "Explain it to us, please."

Mr. Mitchell yawned. "Make it good and make it fast," he said. "I'm getting sleepy, finally."

Jamie and Todd looked at each other.

"Come on," Mrs. Watson said. "You told the crew you'd just 'felt' like taking a boat ride, but we know you two. There had to be more to it than that."

"Okay." Jamie sighed. She was sleepy, too, and she figured they might as well get it over with. "We—"

"Uh...it was my idea," Todd said. "By the way."

Mr. Watson stuffed his hands into his vest pockets. "We don't care whose idea it was. You both went along with it."

"Okay," Jamie said again. "We...I saw the lantern tonight, after the bear rattle fell off the can. And...well, Todd and I have been talking about trying to find out what it was."

Mrs. Mitchell looked confused. "Find out what what was, honey?"

"The lantern, Mom," Todd said. "You know—Ben Tyler, Tyler's Ghost, Tyler's Lantern?"

Mr. Watson looked ready to hit the roof. "Do you mean you got us—not to mention the entire lake crew—out of bed in the middle of the night, worried sick we'd have to dredge the lake, and all the time you were on a ghost hunt? Jamie, I thought you'd outgrown all that!"

"Not a ghost hunt." Todd looked insulted. "We don't believe in ghosts. We just wanted to find out who carries the lantern, that's all."

"Oh, well, that sounds reasonable." Mrs. Watson was definitely being sarcastic.

For a few more seconds, no one said a word. The adults stared at each other, then at Jamie and Todd, then back to each other.

66

Finally, Mr. Watson tried to pretend he had a cough, but Jamie knew he was chuckling, and as soon as everyone else realized it, too, they joined in. Mrs. Watson tried to stop herself by clapping her hands over her mouth, but it didn't work. Her chuckle came out in little squeaks until she finally had to take her hands away and laugh out loud. Mr. and Mrs. Mitchell hung on to each other and gasped for air.

Jamie and Todd weren't sure what to do at first, but after a while, it was impossible not to laugh along. Besides, Jamie figured if everyone else was so amused, she and Todd still had a future to worry about.

Finally, Mr. Mitchell gave a last hoot and shook his head. "I should say I'm surprised, but I'm not, to tell the truth."

"Well, I *am* surprised." Mrs. Watson passed around mugs of tea and a plate of peanut butter cookies. She wasn't furious anymore, but she'd stopped smiling, and Jamie decided that all the laughter was just the laughter of relief. She knew she was right when her mother said, "What we have to do now is decide on the punishment."

Mrs. Mitchell sighed and wiped her eyes. "Yes, I'm afraid we do."

Jamie and Todd stared at the floor like two guilty five-year-olds while the adults discussed the situation. Jamie hated the feeling.

"We can't ground them," Mr. Mitchell said. "After all, we're on vacation, with only eight days left."

"No, but we can partially ground them," Mrs. Watson said. "How about no hiking alone, no using the boats alone, no going into Spruce without one of us along?"

"Good," Mr. Watson said. "All they can do alone is swim." He laughed at himself. "To be honest, I don't relish the idea of spending the next eight days sitting by the lake with them."

Todd's mother sighed again. "I also think they owe the lake people an apology."

"Mom," Todd said, "We did apologize. When we got back."

"That was just in the flurry of the moment," she said. "They were probably too tired to hear you. No, I think you should go to them in person tomorrow and apologize formally."

"Both of you," Mr. Watson said.

Jeremy yawned. "It *is* tomorrow."

"You're right," Mrs. Watson said. "Get to bed, Jeremy."

"How can I? This is my bedroom, and you're all in it."

Everyone laughed again, and then the Mitchells got up to leave. Dave had already nodded off, so Mr. Mitchell carried him. Jamie walked to the door with Todd.

"I'm sorry," she said. "I talked you into sneaking out. I guess it wasn't such a good plan."

"That's okay." Todd shrugged and yawned. "I wanted to go." He grinned at her. "We got close, Jamie. We got real close."

Dear Jamie,

Are you still alive? You've been gone almost a month, and I haven't even gotten a single postcard. Should I be mad or worried?

Jamie smiled even though she felt guilty. Carrie should definitely be mad. If she knew Jamie had started and torn up three letters, she'd be furious, especially if she knew why. They'd never had trouble talking about anything before, whether the subject was boys or parents or their first bras.

Well, anyway, I'm going to take the chance that you're still alive and write you one more letter. Remember I told you about Diane's cousin who was visiting? He turned out to be a real loser. I guess he thought we were all too young for him, because he kept acting like he was Mr. Cool or something. I've decided to forget all about him even though he was gorgeous. Besides, I've got school to think about. Do you realize we'll actually be in high school pretty soon? I can't wait. If you haven't disappeared from the face of the earth, maybe we'll be able to have some classes together.

Jamie laughed, folded the letter, and put it under her beach towel. It was eleven-thirty in the morning, and she'd been sitting by the lake for an hour, trying to decide exactly what to say when she went to apologize. Her mother had brought it up the first thing at breakfast, and she'd been very grumpy, so Jamie knew she wasn't as amused as she had been the night before.

She started to get up to get it over with, changed her mind, stretched out on the towel, and closed her eyes against the sun. Something Carrie had said in the letter was bothering her. The part about school starting soon. She and Todd had talked about the same thing the night before, but Jamie hadn't really thought about it much until then. Vacation was almost over. She would be leaving soon, going home, picking up life where she'd left off. Leaving Sunrise Lake meant leaving Jim.

Jamie sat up again. She didn't want to think about that. Something would work out. She didn't know what, but she wasn't going to worry about it. She had enough to worry about. Her parents were mad at her, and the entire lake crew was probably trying to figure out a way to ban her from ever coming back.

"Hey, Jamie." Todd flopped down beside her. "Did you apologize yet?"

"No. Did you?"

"Yep." Todd answered.

"Well?" Jamie asked, waiting to hear what had happened when Todd visited the lifeguards who had been out the night before.

"Well, what?"

"Well, were they mean?"

"Boy, were they! They gave me twenty lashes. You should see my back." He grinned. "Go on, get it over with, and then we can swim."

Jamie stood up. "You didn't tell them why we were out, did you?"

"Are you kidding? I'm crazy, but not that crazy."

Jamie forced herself to walk to the main cabin. She knew she'd done something wrong, worrying her parents and everybody, but still, it was humiliating to be punished for it, even if the punishment wasn't all that bad. It made her feel like a little girl. She just hoped Jim wasn't there to watch.

He was there. In fact, he opened the door for her. He was grinning, and his dimples were deeper than ever. "Well, Jamie Watson, come on in. We've...ah...we've been expecting you!"

He laughed—Jamie'd never heard him really laugh before; it was a beautiful sound—and held the door wide open for her. All she wanted to do was an about-face, but it was impossible. As she stepped in, she felt her cheeks get hot. She hoped everybody thought it was sunburn.

Inside, Bob and a couple of older men who worked at the lake were sitting in camp chairs, drinking soda, and watching a soap opera on a video cassette player. A woman on the screen was yelling, "Please, please, let me explain!" Jamie sympathized with her immediately.

She cleared her throat. "Umm...I'm Jamie Watson and I just want to tell you—"

The soap opera woman started crying hysterically. Jamie felt like joining her, but then Jim turned the volume

70

down. "Come on, you guys," he said. "Forget this garbage and mind your manners." He smiled at Jamie, and she felt better. For a minute, she'd been afraid that he was more interested in the soap opera than in her.

The rest of the crew was looking at her, finally, and she cleared her throat again. "I came to apologize for last night. I didn't mean to cause you so much trouble. I know you have a lot of...responsibilities, and it wasn't fair to—to take advantage of you like that. It was a dumb thing to do, and I'm sorry." Jamie couldn't think of anything to add, so she stopped. She didn't know where she'd found the words, but when she turned them over in her mind again, she decided they sounded pretty good—sincere, but dignified, not weepy and piercing like the soap opera lady.

Nobody said anything for a moment, then Bob took a toothpick out of his mouth and looked around the room. "Well, guys, what do you think?"

Another man—Jamie recognized him from the rescue boat—chuckled. "I say the whip."

Bob frowned. "No, no, we used that on the boy. I say the rack."

They all laughed, even Jim, and Jamie felt her face get hot again. It was worse than humiliating, having him laugh at her. Then she forced herself to look him in the eyes, and when she saw the sparkle in them and the warm way he was smiling, she stopped blushing. Jim wasn't laughing at *her*. He wasn't even angry with her. He was treating her like...a person and not a child who'd misbehaved. She tried to think of something funny to say, but she couldn't, so she just smiled along with them. Then she turned to leave, but Bob stopped her.

"Wait a minute," he said. "We haven't figured out what to do with you yet."

Jamie decided that Bob was a creep.

Jim laughed again and said, "I've got an idea." He took a few steps toward Jamie and put his hand on her shoulder. "Jamie Watson here has tried twice so far to go the distance. Suppose we do this—either she does it today, right now, or she gives up the right to try." He looked at Jamie. "How does that sound to you? Fair?"

"Not really," Jamie said. "But I can do it anyway. Just give me ten minutes to get someone to row for me."

"Okay, then." Jim took his hand away. "Go for it, Jamie Watson."

Jamie moved slowly and calmly to the door, but the minute she got outside, she sprinted across the beach to Todd as if the pebbles were hot coals.

She didn't really know whether she could do the swim or not, but it didn't matter. What mattered was that Jim thought she could. He hadn't exactly said so, but she just knew that's what he meant. He wanted her to do it—for him—so she would. And he'd be waiting for her when she got back.

Todd saw her coming and jumped to his feet. "Hey, Jamie, what is it? You look ready to fly."

"No, I'm ready to swim." Jamie laughed, grabbed his hand, and tried to pull him along with her. "Come on, let's get the boat. I'm ready to go the distance!"

"Now?"

"Why not?" Jamie tugged at his hand again, but he didn't budge. "Come on, Todd, you said you'd be my coach."

"Geez, Jamie. Is that what those guys in there told you to do?" He gestured toward the lifeguards' cabin, and Jamie saw Jim and Bob and one of the other men standing outside, watching them. She dropped Todd's hand. She didn't want Jim to think that she and Todd were anything more than friends.

"Yes, but so what?" she said. "I want to do it, and anyway, if I do, it'll really show them."

Todd thought a second and then nodded. "Okay, but we're not supposed to take the boat out alone."

"Oh." Jamie had forgotten about that. She was pretty sure her parents would agree to it, but they were in Spruce doing the laundry, and she didn't want to take a chance. "All right. Let's get Jeremy and Dave and make them come with us."

It took a bribe of milkshakes and hamburgers at Taylor's Drugstore to pry the two boys away from the raft they were building, but finally Jamie was in the water, heading for the opposite shore.

She followed her plan of swimming and then floating on her back, but by the time she was only halfway across, she was doing a lot more floating than swimming. She was already tired, she'd swallowed so much water her stomach was churning, and she was beginning to think she couldn't make it.

"Hey, Jamie, you look sick," Jeremy called out to her. "Stop, why don't you?"

Jamie was tempted, but she decided to go just a little farther. Maybe she'd get a second wind. She ignored the Germ's remark. "Does anybody have anything to drink?"

Dave had a small can of cranberry juice, and while Jamie trod water, he opened it and handed it over the side of the boat.

"Thanks." Jamie tried not to drink it all in one gulp. It was warm, and when it hit her stomach she thought she might throw up.

When she clapped her hand over her mouth, everybody in the boat looked the other way. "Jamie, hang on," Todd yelled over his shoulder. "I can just make out those jerks who talked you into this—they're watching. I bet they think you can't do it."

73

Jamie didn't have the energy to tell Todd that Jim wasn't a jerk, but the thought that Bob and the others might actually be rooting for her to fail made her mad. She managed to keep the juice down and handed the can back. "Let's keep going," she said.

From then on, it wasn't exactly easy, but it wasn't as hard as it had been, either. Jamie stopped worrying about going fast and just concentrated on going. When she finally touched the shore and then collapsed into the boat, Todd stood up, took off his T-shirt, and waved it in the air like a victory flag. Jamie was too tired to even wonder if Jim had seen it.

He had, though. He was waiting for her when she got back, just as she knew he'd be, with a big, two-dimple smile on his face. She stepped out of the boat, and then something happened that she hadn't even dreamed of.

Jim walked toward her with his arms out, put them around her, and hugged her to him, actually lifting her off the ground.

"Beautiful, Jamie! I knew you could do it!"

He spun her around and then set her back down. He kept hold of her hands, though, and as far as Jamie was concerned, her feet still hadn't touched the ground.

◦ *Eight* ◦

When Jamie woke up the next morning, she sat up, blinked, and then flopped right back down. The bumpy cot creaked under her weight, as usual, but the way she was feeling, it could have been a downy feather bed. Or maybe a cloud, since she was still floating. She smiled to herself, closed her eyes, and tried to remember every detail of what had happened the day before.

She'd climbed out of the boat, wondering exactly what to say to Jim. How many steps had she taken to him before she realized what he was going to do? Was she smiling? She couldn't remember. She knew she'd started to push her hair behind her ears when she saw him running and knew that he was running toward *her*. Then he put his arms out and pulled her to him, calling her Jamie, not Jamie Watson, and saying she was beautiful.

Jamie grinned, remembering the feel of his arms around her waist and the way he'd kept hold of her hands for at least half a minute after he stopped spinning her around. It was an almost perfect rerun of one of her fantasies about him. It would have been completely perfect if he'd kissed her, but she was ninety-nine percent sure that part would come true, too, soon.

She opened her eyes and stared around the room. It looked different. It was brighter than it ever had been, and even the door blankets looked better, kind of quaint instead of just old. Even the peeling ceiling paint didn't seem so ugly. She grinned again. There was nothing different about the room. There was something different about her. She was in love.

She saw her notebook poking out from under a pile of dirty clothes, got it and a pencil, and crawled back into her sleeping bag. Now, at last, she knew what to say to Carrie.

Dear Carrie,

Yes, I'm still alive! I'm more alive than ever! I know you don't know what I'm talking about. Well, I'm talking about love. His name is Jim. He's a lifeguard here. From the minute I saw him, I felt there was something special between us, and yesterday I found out I was right.

Jamie went on to describe everything that had happened since she first set eyes on Jim. It took her half an hour and four pages, and by the time she reached the part about the previous day's hug, the sun was streaming in the window. She heard her parents moving around in the bathroom and then the kitchen, and after a while, she smelled bacon frying. She was glad it wasn't fish, because she was starving. Maybe love did that to you.

She put the letter into an envelope, got dressed, and joined her family. "Hi, everybody."

76

"Good morning, sunshine." Her father tilted his cheek for a kiss.

Jamie sat down and smiled around the table. Being in love meant being in love with everybody, she decided. Even the sight of Jeremy dumping three spoonfuls of sugar on his cereal couldn't make her say something sarcastic.

Her mother passed her the toast. "You certainly look well rested, Jamie," she said. "Your eyes are shining."

Her father peered at her and nodded. "You're very pretty this morning, honey."

"Thanks." Jamie laughed and reached for the bacon. "I'm feeling great."

"Any particular reason?" her mother asked. "Not that we mind, you understand."

Jamie wasn't sure what to say, but Jeremy, of all people, came to her rescue. "She's feeling great because she did the mile swim."

"You did?" Mr. Watson patted her on the shoulder. "That's terrific!"

"It sure is." Mrs. Watson beamed. "I knew you'd been trying, Jamie, and now you've done it. We're proud of you."

"Thank you." Jamie waited to see if Jeremy was going to mention Jim's hug, but he'd gone back to eating, and she figured he thought it was just a congratulations hug, not a love hug.

"Well, well," her father said, "this calls for a celebration. Let's see—how about a big bonfire tonight?"

"Tonight?" Jamie was almost certain that she and Jim would be busy, but she didn't have quite enough courage to say so.

"Oh, that sounds like fun," her mother said. "I'm sure the Mitchells will enjoy it." She looked at Jamie. "Todd rowed for you, didn't he?"

Jamie nodded and tried to figure out a way to stop the big celebration.

"You forgot to mention that Dave and I went along, too," Jeremy said, "just so you and Todd wouldn't get into trouble for taking the boat out alone. Remember?"

Jamie nodded again. Maybe she should just invite Jim. Except he might want to be alone with her.

"Then you all had a part in it," Mr. Watson said. "This calls for a bigger bonfire. What do you think, Jamie?"

Jamie decided she'd just play it by ear. She and Jim could always get away together, maybe out on the pier, like before. Only this time, they'd do more than watch the stars. She smiled at that thought. "It sounds great," she said.

"Good, then that's settled," Mrs. Watson said. "You be sure to tell Todd."

"Okay." Now that her stomach was full, Jamie was ready to fly again. "Is it okay if I go into Spruce? I have a letter to mail."

"You can't," the Germ said immediately. "You're grounded."

"I know." Jamie turned to her parents. "It's just that I wrote to Carrie, and if I don't mail it today, she won't even get it till after we get home."

"As it happens, I have a couple of postcards to send," her father said. "How about if we walk into town together?" He patted his stomach. "I've been sitting in the boat too much. Give me a chance to shower, and then we'll both get some exercise."

"Okay." Jamie didn't really mind. She had no intention of spending a second longer in Spruce than she had to, anyway. She wanted to be free for Jim when he got off duty.

She told her father she'd meet him at the lake and then ran ahead of him to the bathroom so she could see whether

her eyes really were shining. They were; even the old mirror couldn't hide it. She wondered whether Jim would notice. She wondered what they'd say when they first saw each other. She watched her cheeks get red as she tried to imagine the scene, and then she remembered that he was probably sitting in his chair at that moment, maybe wondering exactly the same thing. Why was she wasting her time in the cabin, building another fantasy, when she could be outside, making it come true?

Jim wasn't in the chair when Jamie got to the lake. Another lifeguard was, and she was disappointed. She'd been so sure that he'd be out there, watching the water but really looking for her. Then she remembered that the three lifeguards were always switching times around. Maybe he had an errand to run, the way she did.

She walked back up to the path that led toward Spruce. She could see the whole beach from there and watch for her father and Jim at the same time.

She saw her father first. He came out of the cabin, spotted her, and waved, then sat down on the porch steps to lace up his hiking boots. Jamie waved back and laughed to herself. He must have forgotten that he didn't need boots to get into Spruce. If he wanted exercise, he should have worn jogging shoes.

While she waited, she scanned the beach again, and that's when she saw Jim. He was in his swimsuit, looking tall and blond and beautiful and tan. He wasn't looking at Jamie, though. His eyes were fastened on the girl beside him, who was also tall and blonde and beautiful. And tan.

Jamie glanced toward her father, who was starting on his second boot. She kept her eyes on him for a few seconds, trying to convince herself that she'd seen double or that the girl was Jim's twin sister. Then she forced herself to turn her head and see the truth.

Jim slipped his arm around the girl's waist, and they walked together toward the pier. The girl looked at the water, then at Jim. They laughed; then he kissed her on the mouth before Jamie could stop looking.

She could hear her father clomping toward her, and when he was almost there, he called, "Okay, all ready for the big trek?"

Jamie kept her eyes on the ground, then made herself look one more time. She saw Jim run back toward the beach. He stopped, turned around, and held out his arms. Jamie didn't wait for the hug. The hug that should have been hers.

She turned away and collided with her father.

"All set?" he said.

"Dad, I just remembered, I promised Todd that I'd go fishing with him this morning, to pay him back for rowing yesterday." Jamie crossed her fingers against the lie and was amazed at how normal her voice sounded. "It completely slipped my mind. Anyway, he's probably wondering where I am, so I'd better get going."

"Well, all right." Her father chuckled. "I guess I can find my way into town alone. Want me to take that for you?"

Jamie looked at the envelope in her hand and shook her head. "No. Thanks, anyway. I want to write a P.S. on it."

She waved good-bye to her father and walked to the cabin without looking back. Her mother and Jeremy were gone. She tore up the letter and stuffed the pieces into her suitcase. Then she grabbed her fishing pole and went to find Todd so she could talk him into going fishing. If he didn't want to, then she'd tell her father that Todd had forgotten, because her father was sure to ask how they did.

When she went out the door, she deliberately looked away from the beach. But halfway to the Mitchells' cabin, she had to stop and turn around. She was facing the lake then, but it didn't matter. She was crying too hard to see anything.

Everyone agreed that the bonfire was the best they'd ever built. Everyone—except Jamie—was laughing and having a great time, piling wood as high as they dared. Mr. Mitchell brought his guitar, and when Mrs. Mitchell suggested that he throw it on the fire, he serenaded her with "You Are My Sunshine."

It was a perfect song to make Jamie cry again, but she was all cried out—for the moment, anyway. She was worn out, too, and she moved around the bonfire like a sleepwalker, actually hoping her mother would notice and ask her what was wrong. Then she could pretend to be sick and go to bed.

Mrs. Watson didn't notice, though. Nobody did, and Jamie figured the cold washcloth she'd kept on her eyes for half an hour had worked. It was too bad there wasn't some version of the cold-washcloth technique she could use on her feelings.

She stared into the bonfire and tried to see pictures in the flames, but the only one that appeared was the one she'd seen that morning, of Jim and his girlfriend, so she closed her eyes.

"Hey, Jamie?"

"What?"

"Your father just asked me how many fish we caught this morning. I told him I forgot that we were supposed to go." Todd grinned. "Was that the right thing to say?"

Jamie nodded. "Thanks."

"That's okay." Todd lowered his voice. "What's the story?"

Jamie sighed. He was acting as though they were little kids with a big secret to hide. "Nothing, really," she said. "I just wanted to get out of walking into Spruce, so I said the first thing that came to my mind."

"Oh." Todd looked disappointed that there wasn't anything more to it than that, and Jamie actually laughed.

"What's so funny?"

"Nothing. I wasn't laughing at you," she said. It was true. She was laughing at herself. She knew she wasn't a little girl anymore—she wasn't sure about Todd—but Jim saw her that way. And she'd known it almost from the beginning. That time she'd been so mad when she saw him on the beach with all the little girls. Part of her had known right away that in Jim's eyes, she was just like them. But she hadn't been able to admit it. And the time before that, when she'd tried to write about him to Carrie. Somehow she knew that there was nothing to write about, but she kept on pretending there was. If she'd just listened to herself then, she knew she wouldn't be feeling what she was feeling now.

"Well, so what are you laughing at?"

"Oh." Jamie had almost forgotten that Todd was there, and she was beginning to wish he'd leave. "Nothing," she said again. "I was just thinking."

"About what?"

She wished he'd stop asking questions. She wanted to scream. "About Tyler's Ghost," she whispered.

Todd's eyes lit up. "Do you have another plan?"

"Not yet," Jamie lied. "But I'm working on it."

"Okay! But don't forget, we've only got five days left, so make it good." Todd nudged her on the shoulder, and then finally he went away.

Jamie had absolutely no "plan" at all about Tyler's Ghost, but at least she'd gotten rid of Todd. The only plan on her mind now was how to get through the next five days.

At first, it seemed as if she couldn't escape the sight of Jim and his girlfriend. Jamie still wasn't allowed to go anywhere by herself except to the beach, and they were always there, laughing and holding hands. When Jim was on duty, his girlfriend planted herself next to his chair and talked up at him. Or else she swam, and Jamie knew that she was the only one he kept his eyes on. People could have drowned by the dozens, and Jim wouldn't have noticed a thing.

She wished it would rain again so they'd all have to stay inside, but the weather didn't cooperate. She could have gone hiking or fishing with her parents or the Mitchells, but she wanted to be by herself, and the only way to do that was to stay in the cabin or go to the beach.

After two days, the girl left. She'd just been visiting Jim. Jamie was glad she didn't have to look at her anymore, but seeing Jim alone again didn't cheer her up, since she knew where his mind was. She knew she had no right to be angry with him, and she wasn't, but just seeing him made her hurt. She didn't even want to have to smile or wave at him, so she finally started spending more time with her parents and even Jeremy. And when she *was* at the beach, she tried never to catch his eye or walk too close to his chair.

It worked for a while, but one day, when she and Todd had raced each other to the raft and back and she'd won, Todd said, "Jamie, I think that lifeguard's trying to get your attention."

Jamie looked and saw Jim waving at her. Todd grinned. "Try not to let him talk you into swimming the lake again, okay?"

She ran up the pier and across the beach. She knew that whatever Jim had to say wouldn't be what she wanted to hear, and she wanted to get it over with.

"Hi, Jamie Watson."

"Hi."

Jim leaned over the side of the chair and smiled down at her. "I just wanted to let you know I put your name in the record book."

"Oh." She was right. That wasn't what she wanted to hear. "Thanks."

"So you've made your mark."

"I guess so." She tried to smile back.

"Now you'll have something to brag about when you get back home," he said. "When are you leaving?"

"In a couple of days."

"Well, good luck, Jamie Watson."

He settled back in his chair, and Jamie went back to the pier. It was the last time she spoke to him before she left.

Since Jamie and her mother always unpacked when they got to the lake, her father and Jeremy always packed up before they went home. That was the deal. But that summer Jamie volunteered to take Jeremy's place, and he was more than happy to let her. She didn't really enjoy packing, but it kept her busy.

By the last night, when the two families had their final cookout together, Jamie was feeling better—not good, but better. Better enough to eat, anyway, and to sing "I Love to Go A-Wandering," with Todd, which their parents insisted on.

While they were roasting marshmallows, Todd said, "Listen, next summer we'll do it."

"Do what?"

"Trap the ghost." He laughed. "After all, we've got almost a whole year to come up with another plan. And don't forget, I'll need you to row when I try the distance."

"Maybe next year we won't want to do that stuff," Jamie said. "I mean, we'll be older, you know. Big-time high school kids."

"Yeah, maybe you're right," he said. "Anyway, that reminds me—Have a good year, okay?"

"Thanks." Jamie started feeling a tiny bit better. Looking ahead, even if she didn't know exactly what was there, was a lot easier than looking back. "You have a great year, too, Todd."

She stuck another marshmallow on her stick and held it over the fire. A little way beyond the flames, she could see the empty lifeguard's chair, and for a minute she couldn't take her eyes from it.

"Hey, Jamie," Todd said. "Your marshmallow just fell off."

Jamie looked, laughed, and reached for another one. She couldn't wait to get home.

Conclusion of Book One

What will happen to Jamie as she gets older? How will she have changed by the time she's seventeen? In what ways will she still be the same? To find out, turn the page to begin Jamie's seventeenth year.

Book Two

Jamie at Seventeen

☀ *One* ☀

*I*t took Jamie almost five minutes to figure out what was different. As soon as she'd walked into the room, she felt that something had changed or was missing, but she couldn't put her finger on what it was. The room looked just as small; the old iron cot was definitely just as saggy. The only change in the "doors" was that the blankets had faded a little bit more. She pulled the closet one aside to hang up her vest and jeans, and that's when she realized what had happened.

"Hey, Mom? You won't believe this, but my room's been painted!"

"You won't believe *this*, but the whole cabin has." Jamie's mother came into the room and stared around. "Everything except the knotty pine is now brand-new beige. And guess what else?"

"What?"

"The bear rattle's gone."

"You're kidding. After all this time?"

"Well, it's not in the cabinet above the stove, where we always stowed it, and I haven't seen it anywhere else, either."

"Maybe the Mitchells have it." Jamie thought a second. "Or Daddy probably found it first and threw it in the lake while nobody was looking."

"No, he wanted to do that last summer, but I wouldn't let him." Mrs. Watson laughed. "It just isn't the kind of thing you throw away."

"I know what you mean." Jamie was staring at the inside wall of her closet. Whoever painted the cabin had slopped some beige over "Watson Was Here," too, but most of the red lettering still showed through, and she was glad. So far, it was the only real mark she'd made in life outside of doing the mile swim. She didn't really think it would be the last mark, but it was nice to know it hadn't disappeared. Besides, she still liked mysteries. "Hey, Mom, did anybody see the lantern the last two summers?"

"What...oh, you mean Tyler's Ghost." Her mother rolled her eyes. "I hope you're not planning another escapade, Jamie. You're almost seventeen now, after all."

"I wasn't planning anything," Jamie said. "I just wondered."

"Well, I think Jeremy is probably the one to ask about it. The summer before last, Todd didn't take much of an interest in it, since you weren't here. And then last year, as you know, Todd wasn't here, either. So Jeremy's the expert on Tyler's Ghost now."

"Good."

Mrs. Watson laughed again and put her arm around Jamie's shoulder as they walked back into the kitchen. "I'm so glad you were able to come with us this summer. We missed you the last two times."

90

"I'm glad, too." Two summers ago, Jamie had actually received permission to stay with Carrie instead of coming to the lake. Her family was only going for two weeks that year, anyway, and she thought she'd have more fun at home. Then, last summer, she'd found a job at a dress shop in the mall. It paid too well to pass up, so she'd stayed with her grandmother. This summer, she couldn't get that job or find another one, either, so she'd decided to come along with her family on vacation. She could always baby-sit for a few weeks when she got back, and a month at Sunrise Lake, with nothing to worry about but sunburn, sounded perfect. "I know what," she said to her mother. "Let's put the rest of the stuff away later and go for a quick hike now, before Daddy and Jeremy get back."

"No, you go ahead." Mrs. Watson took a rag and started wiping out some cabinets. "I'll dust a little while I wait for the Mitchells." She grinned. "Looks like you and Todd will have to build another bear scare if that rattle doesn't turn up."

Jamie tied a blue sweatshirt around her waist and stepped out onto the porch. It still sloped, and the screens still sagged. As she headed toward the lake, she thought that except for a new coat of paint and a missing tin can, nothing had changed much. Before they'd left Denver, she'd presented all her usual arguments for going someplace new and different, and her parents had given all their usual reasons why they couldn't, but this summer, Jamie didn't mind so much. This was her last high school summer. Next year, she'd *have* to work to save for college. There might not be another summer, ever again, when she could just do nothing but swim and read and sleep late and just let the days go by that way. She was glad to be back at Sunrise Lake.

She reached her father and Jeremy just as they were climbing out of the rowboat. "Hi, guys."

"Jamie!" Mr. Watson reached down and patted the boat. "How do you like it? A beauty, right?"

Jamie looked. It was gray. The last time she'd been there, they'd had a blue one. Except for the color, they were exactly alike. She laughed. "It's terrific, Dad."

Jeremy looked disgusted. "What do you care? You don't like fishing, anyway. You won't even eat them."

"That was three years ago," Jamie said.

"Big deal."

Most of the time now, Jamie could get along with her brother, but every once in a while, he drove her crazy. He was twelve; he griped a lot; and when he wasn't griping, he was usually sulking about something. "You know, Germ," she said, "you're turning into a very belligerent kid."

Mr. Watson gave a time-out signal. "Speaking of belligerence, let's not have any of it, okay?"

"She started it."

For a second, Jamie felt like pushing him in the lake. Usually, those feelings lasted longer, so she figured she must be improving. "Look, Jeremy, I'll make a deal with you. If you catch more fish than I do this summer, I promise I'll never call you Germ again, even if you act like one."

Jeremy shrugged as if he didn't care, but Jamie knew how much he hated the nickname. "Okay," he said. "At least it'll be an easy bet to win."

Jamie left them with the boat and walked onto the pier. When she got to the end of it, she turned around and looked back over the beach, toward the lifeguard's chair. She had to do a double take before she realized that the boy sitting in it wasn't Jim. He looked so much like him that she almost expected him to wave and say, "Hi, Jamie

Watson!" and then flash his dimples at her. Three summers earlier, she'd practically lived for the sight of him, but it seemed even longer than that.

She walked slowly back up the pier and onto the beach, remembering how that summer's ending had nearly ruined the beginning of high school. She'd moped around for so long that Carrie finally threatened to disown her as a friend.

"Look, this is getting disgusting," Carrie had told her. "Everybody has crushes that don't go anywhere. He was probably a creep, anyway."

"Maybe," Jamie said, "but I'm just so mad at myself. I think I knew that nothing would even happen and that he wasn't really interested in me. But I still went around like an idiot, pretending it would."

"I know. But look, this is just the beginning."

Jamie groaned. "Is that supposed to cheer me up?"

"No, I mean the beginning of boys," Carrie said. "We're just starting high school. Then there's college. So wait. You'll find someone."

Jamie stooped over and picked up a handful of rocks, then walked along the lake's edge, trying to skip them over the water. All but one sank without a skip. She still couldn't do that very well.

She still didn't deal with boys all that well, either, but she was getting better. Even her first date in high school wasn't as much of a disaster as she thought it would be. It was a girl-asks-boy dance, and Jamie had waited until she was ninety-nine percent certain she wouldn't be turned down before she invited anybody. Gary Simpson had been smiling at her in English class and sitting near her at lunch for three weeks straight. Jamie figured she wouldn't make a fool of herself by asking him, and she'd been right— he'd gone to the dance with her. Gary was good-looking, but he was also about as interesting as an empty spool of thread. He didn't like to read; he didn't like to swim; he didn't even like to eat. He liked *her*, she guessed, but after a few more dates, that wasn't enough.

After that, she'd dated a few more boys—not half as many as Carrie—but she still hadn't "found" anyone. Maybe she wasn't looking hard enough.

"Maybe you're looking *too* hard," Carrie had said. "There are plenty of other things to think about besides boys, you know."

Jamie knew that. But she wasn't really thinking about "boys"; she was thinking about falling in love. That's what she hadn't found yet.

As she passed the lifeguard's chair, she glanced up. The new guard was squinting out at the water, so she couldn't tell if his eyes were blue or not, and he wasn't smiling, so she didn't know if he had dimples, but it didn't matter. He was a true "Jim clone."

Jamie wasn't the same Jamie, though, and she was pretty positive she wouldn't find love waiting for her in a Sunrise Lake lifeguard chair. So she kept on walking, right into the path of a flying Frisbee, which hit her square in the stomach.

"Sorry about that." A girl about Jamie's age came running over to get the Frisbee. She picked it up and smiled.

"That's okay," Jamie said. "I wasn't looking where I was going."

"Yeah, I don't blame you." The girl glanced back at the lifeguard and lowered her voice. "He's gorgeous, isn't he? I've had my eye on him since I got here."

"Well...good luck." Jamie laughed and decided not to give the girl any warnings about false expectations. "How long are you staying?"

"A few weeks. My name's Cindy, by the way."

"I'm Jamie. It's nice to find somebody else my age here."

"Well, my brother's only a year younger than I am—I'm sixteen—and I met a couple of other kids, too." Cindy twirled the Frisbee on one finger. "Maybe we can all do stuff together, and it won't be as boring as I thought it would be."

"That sounds great." Jamie had never really been bored at the lake, but still, it would be nice to have other people besides her family and the Mitchells to do things with. "I have to get back to my cabin now," she said, "but I'll see you tomorrow, okay?"

"Okay, good." Cindy ran up the beach toward a boy who was waiting for her with his hands on his hips. They both had the reddest hair and the whitest skin Jamie had ever seen, and she figured they had to be brother and sister.

She waved as she passed them and then broke into a run on the way back to the cabin. It was only about four o'clock in the afternoon. The Mitchells probably hadn't come yet, but she knew her mother expected some help getting everything ready for the "reunion" cookout. Besides, she was starving.

Mrs. Watson was making hamburger patties when she got there. "Here." She handed Jamie a roll of aluminum foil. "You can wrap the ears of corn in this. Don't shuck them, either."

"Why not?"

"Your father wants to roast them in the coals."

"But the last time we did that they burned."

Mrs. Watson shrugged. "Well, you know Daddy. He keeps trying every year."

Jamie looked around. "Where is he, anyway?" She found a bag of potato chips to munch on and started wrapping the corn.

"Outside somewhere, trying to cheer Jeremy up."

"What's wrong with Jeremy?"

95

"He's twelve years old." Mrs. Watson raised her eyebrows and sighed. "He's slightly moody."

"Tell me about it."

"Well, you shouldn't have any trouble relating to that." Her mother laughed. "That summer you and Todd snuck out on the boat, you went through moods the way you used to go through diapers."

"I guess I did." When Jamie had finally told her mother about Jim—two weeks after they had gotten home—her mother had surprised her by taking the whole thing seriously. It hadn't helped the way she felt about Jim, but it *had* helped the way she felt about her mother, and they were like good friends now. "Don't tell me the—Jeremy's interested in a girl."

"Not *a* girl, just girls in general. At least he's thinking about being interested, and I'm pretty sure he's scared to death." Mrs. Watson put the stacks of hamburgers into the refrigerator and took out a package of hot dogs. "Jeremy doesn't really have any friends who are girls, and he doesn't know quite how to act. You've had Todd as a friend since you were about three years old, so you got a chance to find out that the opposite sex is human, too."

"Well, pretty soon he can hang out with Dave and forget about everything else. Or they can both be moody together."

Mrs. Watson laughed. "Thank goodness for the Mitchells."

The Mitchells arrived about an hour later. Jamie was in her room, putting things away, when she heard her parents shout their greetings. She ran her fingers through her short hair and went outside to join them.

Mrs. Mitchell was carrying what looked like about fifteen pies and couldn't hug her, but Mr. Mitchell put his arms around her and said, "Jamie! You're all grown up!"

Mrs. Mitchell peered around the pies. "Oh, my, she certainly is! Todd," she called, "come out here and say hello to Jamie. See if you recognize her." She turned back to Jamie and laughed. "He's been driving for the last three hours. You'd think he would have been the first one out of the car."

Jamie watched as a tallish boy with thick brown hair slid out from behind the steering wheel of the Mitchells' dusty station wagon. He touched his toes a couple of times, then straightened up and walked over to the rest of them. He was a little taller, a little broader in the shoulders, than the last time she'd seen him, but she didn't have any trouble recognizing Todd, at least not from the way he looked.

The way he acted was something else, though. He shook hands with everyone, but he didn't say much, and when he got to her, he just gave her a quick smile and a "Hi, Jamie." Then he went back and started unloading the car.

Jamie had been looking forward to seeing him. After all, it had been three years, and she was curious to find out whether he had changed. She thought that he'd be glad to see *her*, or at least curious, too, but he didn't act happy or curious. He acted as if she were invisible.

❅ *Two* ❅

"I don't know what woke me up," Mrs. Watson said, "but when I couldn't get back to sleep, I decided to make a cup of tea. I looked in on Jamie, and that's when I discovered that she was gone."

Jeremy nudged Jamie in the side. "You forgot to stuff a bunch of clothes in your sleeping bag to make it look like you were still there. That was your big mistake."

"*Now* you tell me." Jamie laughed and reached for another hot dog. "I'll keep it in mind for the next time."

"Oh, no!" Mr. Watson tried to sound serious. "There isn't going to be any next time." He stared at Jeremy. "Don't you get any ideas, either."

"Or you," Mr. Mitchell said to Dave. "I'll never forget the moment we discovered the boat was missing. We thought Jamie and Todd had drowned."

"It was the worst moment of my life." Mrs. Mitchell shook her head sadly and stared into the campfire. Then she started to smile. "And to think, all that time we were worried sick, they were off hunting a ghost, happy as clams."

Jamie bit into her hot dog and laughed with everybody else. The reunion cookout was following its usual routine. They'd eaten until they were stuffed—except for the charred corn—and caught up on everything that had happened over the year. (Jamie and Todd had just finished their junior year in high school, Jeremy and Dave were both wearing glasses now, Mr. Mitchell had lost his job but found a better one, and Mrs. Watson was thinking of retiring); and then it was time for reminiscing.

They went over all the old stories about things they'd done at Sunrise Lake, but they saved the "Great Ghost Hunt" for last. Jamie had a feeling it would be the favorite for a long time unless Jeremy or Dave did something to top it.

"At least we can laugh about it now," Mrs. Mitchell said.

"We laughed about it *then*. We were too tired and sleepy to stay mad." Mr. Mitchell chuckled and started strumming his guitar. "I wonder what those two have planned for this summer."

"I'm not sure I want to know," Mrs. Watson said.

Jamie finished her hot dog and looked at Todd. He was sitting with his hands jammed into the pockets of his windbreaker, staring at the fire. He'd hardly said three words to her or anyone else.

Jamie felt funny about it. A lot had happened since they'd seen each other last two summers earlier, and she knew that since she'd changed, Todd must have, too. She didn't expect them to become instant buddies again, but he was acting as if she were a stranger.

99

After the way he'd treated her when he first got there and the way he was treating her now, Jamie was almost ready to get mad. But then she thought maybe it was the way their parents were acting. The adults made all kinds of remarks about how grown-up Jamie and Todd were, but Jamie knew they still thought of them as the two little kids who hunted snakes and got lost together. It was a little embarrassing. She and Todd were seventeen now. They couldn't exactly take their pails and shovels and play together the way they did when they were five.

Mr. Mitchell was trying to find the right fingering on his guitar, and Jamie realized that she and Todd were going to be asked to sing. She also realized that Todd wasn't in the mood for it, so she decided to help him out.

"I know what's coming now," she said. "You want a famous Todd and Jamie duet, right?"

"Right," Mr. Mitchell said. "And don't try to weasel out of it, either."

"I don't want to weasel out of anything. But I was just thinking, this might be the last time we ever sing together, so we want to be perfect. Give us some time to practice, okay?"

"Uh-oh." Jeremy groaned. "She wants perfection. That means we'll all be here forever."

Jamie gave him a soft punch on the shoulder. "Have you caught any fish yet?"

"How could I? We just got here."

"Then we're still even, Germ." She grinned at her brother and turned back to the rest of them. "I don't know about Todd, but my voice isn't in amazing shape right now; not that it ever was. But I promise you'll have a song out of us before the vacation's over. Okay, Todd?"

Todd stuffed his hands deeper into his pockets and nodded. "Fine with me."

"Well, all right," Mrs. Watson said. "But while they're getting their act together, let's at least have some music."

Mr. Mitchell worked his way through about fifteen songs, getting better as he went along, and everyone joined in except Dave, who was chewing on his tenth marshmallow, and Todd, who kept his mouth closed and his eyes on the fire.

Jamie was beginning to wonder if her "negotiations" had been worth it when she caught him looking at her. While everyone else was struggling to reach a high note, Todd mouthed the word "thanks."

Jamie mouthed back "you're welcome" and went on singing. They might not be buddies anymore, but maybe they could be friends.

"Jamie?"

"Yes, Mom?"

"What are your plans for today?"

"I'm not sure." Jamie bent close to the bathroom mirror and rubbed some sunscreen on her face. She'd given up ever trying to get a tan. "I thought I'd see if Todd wants to go swimming, for starters."

"Oh, that's a good idea. And afterward you can both join his parents and me. We'll be on that trail to the bluff."

"Okay. Where are Dad and Jeremy?"

"They're fishing on the boat, with Dave." Mrs. Watson poked at the blanket door of the bathroom. "See you later."

"Okay. Have fun."

Jamie climbed up on the wooden stool and stared at her bottom half in the mirror. Her legs were still long, but the rest of her seemed to fit with them now, and her knees didn't look quite so knobby.

Back on the floor, she decided that her new haircut was the best possible choice. The year before she'd tried to grow it long, but she gave up before it even reached her shoulders, because it was so scraggly she looked like a scarecrow. Now it was short again, but it was cut so well that all she had to do was shake her head and it fell into place. Her hair would never be blonde even if she spent the rest of her life in the sun, but at least her eyes would always be blue. Her new swimsuit (green this time, with very strong straps) made them almost aqua.

She thought she looked better than she ever had, but Carrie told her she had always looked good and just finally realized she didn't have to spend two hours in front of a mirror fretting about it.

It would have been nice if there was someone—a boy, to be specific—she wanted to look good *for*, but until there was, the least she could do was please herself.

She pulled on a short white terry-cloth beach robe, took a towel, and headed over to the Mitchells' cabin. Todd was sitting in one sagging wicker porch chair. His feet were propped up on another one, and his face was buried in a book.

Jamie tapped the door. "Hey, Todd. Hi."

Todd got up slowly and came over. "Hi, Jamie." He looked at her through the screen. "What's up?"

"Nothing. I just thought you might want to go swimming." Jamie laughed. "We're big kids now, so we don't have to take the test. We can just plunge right in." She pointed at the book. "You didn't really come all the way to Sunrise Lake to read on your first day here, did you?"

Todd glanced down at the book as if he'd never seen it before. "Oh. No, I guess not." He scratched his head and yawned. "I'm not sure I'm ready to swim yet, though. Maybe later, okay?"

"Sure, okay." Jamie started to turn away and then stopped. "Do you feel as funny as I do?"

"What do you mean?"

"I mean having our parents treat us like three-year-olds. It's a little embarrassing the way they expect us to become instant friends again. At least it is for me." Jamie felt even more embarrassed then, trying to explain herself through the screen door, especially since Todd wasn't giving her any help, but she kept going. "And I thought you felt that way, too, last night." She blushed and laughed. "Anyway, I promise not to make you sneak out of your cabin if you promise not to come up with any crazy schemes."

"No crazy schemes." Todd smiled. "That's a promise I think I can keep. Maybe I'll see you later, Jamie."

"All right. 'Bye."

Jamie left the cabin and headed toward the lake. What was the matter with him, anyway? He hadn't even opened the door to her. And he'd smiled as if it had cost him something. The night before, she thought they still had something in common because of the way he had thanked her about the singing, but now she wasn't so sure.

She kicked a few pebbles and watched them scatter in front of her. Maybe she was just overreacting. She still tended to do that. Todd was probably just tired from driving so much. She remembered the way he'd touched his toes when he got out of the car, and she giggled. Or maybe he still wasn't a very good swimmer and didn't want her to show him up.

She walked down the beach and immediately spotted Cindy and her brother and two other boys near the lifeguard's chair. She waved to Cindy and started over to them. At least there was someone around who wanted to have fun.

"Hi, Jamie!" Cindy glanced back at the lifeguard and then trotted over. "I've been hanging out by his chair for an hour. I don't think he's getting my message."

Jamie grinned. "I know the feeling."

"Try drowning," Cindy's brother said. "That'll get his attention."

"Very funny." Cindy pointed to Jamie. "This is Jamie. Jamie, this is my brother, Rick." She ran her hands through her blazing hair. "What do you mean, you know the feeling?"

Jamie started to think up a lie and then laughed at herself. What difference did it make now? "Oh, the summer I was fourteen I had a big thing for one of the lifeguards here," she said. "He didn't get *my* message, either."

"You must know the place pretty well," Rick said.

Jamie nodded. "Sure. I've been coming here almost every summer since I was three. What do you want to know?"

"What there is to do," Cindy said, "besides throw a Frisbee."

"Well, you can fish or row. Or you can go the distance."

"What's that?"

"Swim across the lake. It's a little over a mile. If you do it, you get your name in a record book. I did it. It's kind of a challenge, I guess." Jamie squinted across the lake and decided not to tell them the real reason she'd done it.

"I might give that a try," Rick said.

"Not me." Cindy looked at Jamie. "Oh, I forgot. Come on and meet the other kids I told you about. Hey, if you know this place so well, maybe we can plan a big hike or something before we leave. You know, get up really early, have breakfast on the trail, and keep on going all day."

"That won't be hard," Jamie said as they walked across the sand. "There are enough trails around here to keep us going for weeks."

The other kids turned out to be two sixteen-year-old brothers. They were twins, and their names were Matt and Mark, so Jamie immediately dubbed them "M&M," but she kept that to herself. They were okay, she decided, but definitely not her type.

They all swam for a while, and when Jamie mentioned Spruce and the hamburgers they could get at Taylor's Drugstore, everybody wanted to hike in and eat lunch.

As she walked back to the cabin to change, Jamie kept an eye out for Todd, but he wasn't around. For some reason, she had felt funny all morning, swimming without him and now going into town without him. They'd always done everything together, and she kept expecting him to turn up, nudge her with his elbow, and start hatching some plan or other. Then she remembered that he'd spent a whole summer there without her. Maybe he'd gotten used to hanging out by himself. In the old days, she would have felt much more comfortable with him than with Cindy and Rick and M&M, but this summer she felt as if she didn't know Todd any better than she knew them.

She did know the way into Spruce, though, and when they got there, she was glad to see that it hadn't changed at all. Even Mr. Taylor was still there and still remembered her.

After they ate, the others wandered around the little town, but Jamie stayed behind at the drugstore, checking out the magazine and paperback racks. They were only about half full, as usual, but she found a mystery book and then discovered that Mr. Taylor still carried the lemon-scented shower splash she'd bought the last time she was there. When she opened it and sniffed, she half expected to see Jim come walking through the door, knocking her off her feet with his blond hair and sexy voice. He didn't, but she bought the splash, anyway. She liked the smell of it, whether she was in love or not.

It was about three o'clock when they got back to the lake. Jamie said good-bye to the others and walked down to where her father and the two boys were just tying up the boat.

"How'd you do?"

"She asks how we did." Mr. Watson slapped both boys on the back. "Go ahead. Show her."

Dave held up a line with two fish dangling from it, and Jeremy opened the creel and showed her three more. "The two big ones are mine," Jeremy said proudly.

"No need to rub it in," Mr. Watson said. "You're forgetting who taught you everything you know."

"That's two for me, Jamie." Jeremy grinned. "You'd better get started, or you'll lose certain name-calling privileges."

"Don't worry," Jamie said. "I haven't forgotten. Just give me time."

She picked up her father's tackle box, and they started walking toward the cabins. As they got close to the pier, she saw someone doing laps between it and the raft.

"That looks like Todd," she said.

"It is." Dave stopped beside her. "I guess he finally remembered there's things to do here besides sit in the cabin all day and be grouchy."

Jamie laughed. "Why *is* he acting so grouchy? Is something wrong?"

"I don't know." Dave shrugged. "Nobody tells me anything."

They started walking again, and when Jamie looked back, Todd was still in the water, swimming back and forth.

☼ Three ☼

Dear Carrie,

Greetings from Sunrise Lake! I bet you can't believe I'm writing you an actual letter when I've only been here a week. Well, I am, and it isn't because I don't have anything else to do, either, so don't get insulted. I miss you.

Jamie planted her hand on the note pad and waited until a gust of wind from the lake stopped curling the paper over her pen. She really did miss Carrie.

Anyway, this is the same old place, but I like it a lot better than I used to. There are a few other kids our age here, and we've all been hanging out together. There's even a lifeguard who's an exact double for the one who broke my heart three years ago! He sits in his chair looking beautiful, and one of the girls I met has her eye on him. In case you're getting worried, I don't. Have my eye on him, that is.

Jamie stopped writing and looked up. For a moment her eyes rested on Todd, who was doing laps again between the pier and the raft. His swimming style had improved, she noticed, but it seemed to be his only form of recreation.

Do you remember my "summertime sidekick," Todd? He's back, too. I guess I didn't know him as well as I thought, because he sure has changed—into a real grouch. A nice-looking grouch, but a grouch. He doesn't want to have anything to do with anybody, and he's almost as bad as the Germ in a sulk. I'm beginning to think it's a case of delayed adolescence. I read somewhere that girls grow up faster than boys, but this is ridiculous!

Jamie stopped and looked down the beach at Todd again. He had hauled himself up onto the pier and was standing alone. She had almost decided that if that was the way he wanted to be, that was the way she'd leave him. But seeing him there, staring at the water, she thought maybe she'd give it one more try.

She put her notebook under the towel, then trotted across the sand and onto the slippery boards. "Hi."

"Oh, Jamie, hi." Todd picked a towel up and started drying off.

"Are you just working out, or are you practicing to go the distance?"

"I'm not sure." He actually looked confused. "I guess I'll just see how it goes and then decide."

"Well, if you do decide to swim the lake, I'll be glad to row for you."

"Thanks." Todd grinned, and for a second his dark eyes lit up the way Jamie remembered. "I guess you do owe me one."

"That's true. We had to go through a broken strap and two speedboats before I finally made it." Jamie felt as if they were finally communicating. "Listen, some other kids and I are going on a hike in a couple of days, up to Green's Peak. I'm supposed to be the leader, since I know the trails so well, but I keep having nightmares about getting us all lost." She laughed. "So I thought you might want to help me plan the route. And come along, too, naturally. We could decide what duet to do when our parents finally force us into it."

Todd draped the towel around his shoulders and shook his head. "I don't think so, Jamie."

Jamie waited for him to explain why, and when he didn't, she was so surprised that all she could think of to say was "Oh."

"Your mother knows the area as well as we do—probably better. Why don't you ask her to help you out?"

Jamie stared at him for a second and then said, "Thanks. I guess I will." Then she turned, walked off the pier, and left him alone.

Of course she could ask her mother. That wasn't the point. She'd invited Todd because she thought they were friends, because she thought he'd have fun, but fun didn't seem to be in his vocabulary anymore. Jamie felt like stomping, she was so angry, but by the time she reached her towel, she was calm again. She could hardly pick a fight with him just because he didn't want to go hiking. If he didn't want to, he didn't have to. People changed, and Todd had just happened to change into someone she didn't particularly want to know.

She smeared some more lotion on her face, fished out her note pad, and was chewing on the pen when Cindy appeared.

"Jamie, guess what?" Her red hair was glowing, and so was her face. "I finally managed to talk to Steve, and since the day after tomorrow is his day off, he's coming with us. Isn't that fantastic?" She took a deep breath.

"Who's Steve?"

"Oh, didn't I tell you?" Cindy lowered her voice even though there was no one within twenty feet of them. "Steve's the lifeguard."

There were three lifeguards at Sunrise Lake, as usual, but Jamie knew immediately which one Cindy was talking about. "Are you sure his name's not Jim?"

"No, it's Steve!" Cindy looked ready to burst. "He's eighteen, he's from Idaho, I think he said, he's taking a year off before he goes to college, and when I told him about the hike, he just sort of invited himself."

Jamie laughed. "You sure found out a lot about him in one conversation."

"And it wasn't easy, either. He doesn't talk much." Cindy shook her head and sighed. "But he sure looks great, doesn't he?"

Jamie leaned back and rolled casually on her side so she could get a good view of Steve. Cindy was right. He did look great. But she'd decided that most lifeguards looked great. Maybe it was because they were usually so high up you had to tilt your head to see them, as if you were looking at a statue of a tall Greek god carved in stone.

Steve was gorgeous, but he was also one more person Jamie would be responsible for on the hike. She put off finishing her letter so she could find her mother. She didn't want to lead any Greek god off a cliff.

Mrs. Watson glanced up from the map that was spread out on the wobbly kitchen table. "Did you remember to tell everyone to bring an extra pair of socks?"

"Yes. Cindy and Rick are bringing breakfast, and M&M said they'd supply lunch."

"What about you?" Jeremy asked.

"Matches and the map." Jamie looked at her mother. "How long do you think it'll take us to get to Green's Peak?"

"That depends on which trails you take. There are plenty to choose from, so do you want it easy or hard?"

"Easy." Jamie laughed. "What I really want is not to get lost." She sat back and made a mental checklist of supplies as her mother bent over the table and started tracing an easy route in green magic marker.

Mr. Watson looked up from his book on trout fishing. "I'm not so sure I like this whole idea."

"Why not, Daddy?"

"A bunch of kids, without an adult along in case there's trouble?" He shook his head. "It could be dangerous."

Mrs. Watson looked up. "Don't forget, *I'm* mapping the trail. I'll make sure it's safe. Besides, Jamie's not a kid. She's an experienced hiker. She knows her way around these mountains, and so does Todd, for that matter."

"Um...Todd's not coming," Jamie said.

"He's not? Why not?" Mrs. Watson looked indignant. "You *did* ask him, didn't you?"

"Sure I did." Jamie shrugged. "He just didn't want to come, that's all." She thought a second and then said, "He doesn't want to do anything these days."

"What do you mean?"

"I mean he just wants to be by himself."

"You two have been friends for a long, long time," Mr. Watson said. "You should make an effort to include him in your plans."

"I have, Dad. He just doesn't want to be included." Jamie turned back to her mother. "Let's forget about him, okay?" She pointed to the map. "Let's concentrate on getting us to Green's Peak and back without any broken legs."

Two mornings later, they all gathered outside Jamie's cabin at a quarter to six. What Jamie really felt like doing was crawling back into a warm bed, and she could tell by their yawns and shivers that the others did, too. Only Steve looked awake. He didn't say anything, but at least his eyes were wide open. She noticed that they were pale gray.

Actually, no one talked very much for the first half hour or so. The trail took them through woods so thick they couldn't see the sky. The pines smelled wonderful, but they didn't let in enough light to wake anybody up.

Finally, though, the trees thinned out, and everyone started to come alive.

"Hey, look," Rick said, "sunshine! I think I may make it, after all."

"Just wait," Jamie said. "We haven't even started climbing yet."

"Climbing?" Cindy's face was already beginning to match her hair. "I was sort of hoping we could eat before we started scaling any cliffs."

"Don't worry, I was just kidding. There aren't any cliffs on this route." Jamie turned around and was surprised to see Steve right behind her. "We'll get to a nice clearing in a few minutes," she said to him. "There's a stream that's just beautiful, and I thought we could eat there."

He smiled. "Fine with me."

Jamie smiled, too, and then laughed when she noticed that M&M, who were bringing up the rear, had already dug into their packs and almost finished a bag of potato chips. "They brought the lunch," she whispered to Steve. "Let's hope there's something left by the time we want it."

He laughed, and when the trail widened, he started walking alongside her. "Cindy told me you're a regular at Sunrise Lake."

"I guess I am," Jamie said. She couldn't help noticing that his hair was the exact color of Jim's. "What about you?"

"No, this is my first time here."

"Do you like it?"

He started to shake his head and then stopped. "To be honest, I'm so busy I haven't had a chance to find out."

Jamie laughed. "Lifeguards get time off, don't they?"

"Sure, but I've got a couple of other jobs, too—I'm on the maintenance crew here, and I work at the restaurant in Spruce every night." He picked up a pine cone and turned it around in his hand. "I want to earn as much money as I can for college."

"Oh, that's right. Cindy said you're taking a year off." Jamie smiled. "I thought maybe it was just for fun."

He shook his head. "No, I've *got* to work first. I think I might have a job in Aspen over the winter. Hope so, anyway."

"That's great," Jamie said. "I mean, not that you have to work but that you're doing it."

"Oh, I don't mind. I might even put off school for a second year. I get to travel around a little, see some new places, meet people." Steve pulled aside a broken branch and smiled at her. "Meet you."

Jamie ducked under the branch and tried to think of something clever to say to that, but she couldn't. Steve didn't seem to expect her to, anyway, so it was all right. Besides, she was flattered.

"Hey, Jamie?" Rick came puffing up behind them. "Are we getting close to the dining room?"

"We're there," Jamie said. "Can't you hear the water?"

"All I can hear is my stomach rumbling."

"Guess what?" Cindy and the twins joined them as they walked down to the stream. "We just saw a deer— it was absolutely beautiful!"

"I guess it didn't think *we* were, though," Matt said. "It ran off before I'd blinked twice."

"Hey, this is a great way to work up an appetite," Mark said. "What's for breakfast?"

Cindy and Rick pulled out ham and cheese sandwiches and a big thermos of hot chocolate. After they ate, Cindy walked with Jamie a little way. "Well, what's he like?" she whispered.

"I don't really know yet," Jamie whispered back. "We talked about his jobs, mostly. I guess you could say he's a hard worker."

"I think he's interested in you," Cindy said. She looked disappointed but not exactly heartbroken. "You're the only one he's really talked to much."

"I think it's too early to tell," Jamie said. "Let's see what happens."

What happened was that Steve stayed by Jamie's side for most of the day, except when it was physically impossible, and even then, he was either behind her or in front of her, taking her hand as they cautiously made their way across a fallen tree fifteen feet above a stream or helping her climb over some rocks.

For Jamie, the whole thing felt slightly unreal. Three summers before, she'd eaten and slept with the hope that a certain lifeguard would pay this kind of attention to her, and now it was happening without her even asking for it, like a dream that would come back to her in bits and snatches. Same place, just a different name.

They reached Green's Peak about one o'clock. Everyone was so hungry and tired that they ooh'd and ah'd at the view for just a second and then walked back down the slope a little way to find shelter from the wind.

M&M got a fire going faster than anyone Jamie had ever seen. "You guys must be eagle scouts or something."

Mark laughed and started hauling out enough hot dogs for a small army. "We like to eat, too, you may have noticed."

"I'm all for that," Cindy said. "I never thought I could be so hungry." She stuck a hot dog on a stick and smiled at Steve. "Are you glad you came along, or are you worn out?"

"No, I'm used to this," Steve said. "Besides, I'm enjoying the company." He smiled back, and when he turned to get a hot dog for himself, Cindy rolled her eyes at Jamie.

After they ate, Steve and Jamie walked back up to the top of the peak for a really long look at the view.

"It's beautiful, isn't it?" she said. "I don't think I could ever live in a place that didn't have mountains."

Steve kept staring at the valley below, his hands in his pockets and his hair blowing in the wind. "You're a real nature girl, aren't you?"

It was a line straight out of a three-year-old dream, and Jamie got that unreal feeling again. "I suppose I am," she said. "But then you must be, too."

"Me?"

"Sure. I mean, you took a job in the mountains. You could be working in a library."

"Not enough money," he said.

Jamie laughed. "Some nature lover you are." Then she shivered. "I love the mountains, but I always forget how cold it can be up here, even in the middle of the summer. Let's get out of the wind."

They started back down the slope to help the others clean up. Jamie slipped on some loose rocks, and Steve took her hand to steady her. "I think I'm beginning to like Sunrise Lake," he said. He kept hold of her hand. "I don't have a whole lot of free time, but I was hoping you

115

might like to spend a little of that time with me. It could be fun."

Jamie wasn't listening to his words very closely. She was too busy enjoying the way her hand felt in his. There was absolutely nothing unreal about that.

◦ *Four* ◦

*T*wo days later, Jamie spread her towel out on the beach again, sat down, and picked up the unfinished letter to Carrie.

Skim over everything else I already wrote and answer this question— Is it possible to live out a fantasy? It better be, because I think I'm doing it.

No, wait. Don't skim over the part about the life-guard—the one the girl has her eye on. Guess who the lifeguard has his eye on? If you guess me, you win, and I'll buy the pizza when I get home!

Jamie chewed the pen and thought a minute. If she had to be honest, she'd admit to Carrie that Steve hadn't done more than wave to her since they'd come back from the hike. Maybe she was imagining the whole thing. No, she wasn't. Maybe she hadn't learned much about boys in the last three years, but she could tell when a boy was interested in her. And Steve was. Suddenly, a shadow crossed the page and made her look up.

"Hi, Jamie."

"Hi, Cindy." Jamie felt slightly uncomfortable. Cindy was interested in Steve, after all, and it must have been impossible for her to ignore the fact that he wasn't returning the compliment.

Cindy didn't seem upset, though. She plopped down beside Jamie and smiled. "Guess what?"

"What?"

"I've given up on Steve." She shook her head and laughed. "When I saw him holding your hand the other day, I decided he was a lost cause."

"Oh. Well." Jamie wasn't sure what else to say. "I'm sorry."

"Don't be sorry. It's obvious that he likes you. Do you like him?"

"So far," Jamie said. "I don't know him very well yet, though."

"Sure, but it's not as if you have to fall in love to have a good time."

"I guess not. But it sure would be nice to have both." Jamie leaned back on her elbows. "Anyway, I'm glad you're not upset about Steve."

"Don't worry," Cindy said. "He's cute, but there are other boys around."

Jamie grinned. "Plenty of fish in the lake, right?"

"Right." Cindy pointed. "Like him."

Jamie looked and saw Todd walking down the path toward the beach. He glanced around, and when he saw her, he raised his hand, waved, and headed her way.

"You know him?" Cindy almost squeaked.

"Sort of," Jamie said. She decided not to say that Todd might be a lost cause, too. "Stick around, and I'll introduce you."

"I'm not going anywhere."

They watched as Todd stepped off the path and onto the rocky sand. He moved easily, Jamie noticed, and his hair was already a shade lighter because of the sun. She was still jealous about his hair.

When he reached them, he smiled. "How was the hike?"

"We all survived," Jamie said. "Except for a few blisters, it was great."

"It was fantastic," Cindy said. "If we'd known you were here, we would have asked you to come."

Todd smiled at Jamie again. "Maybe next time."

"Fine," Jamie said. She introduced the two of them and listened with one ear while Cindy chatted about the lake and the mountains and her dream of becoming a cheerleader the following year. She knew Cindy wasn't going to leave unless Todd did, and he had planted himself on the sand as if he were ready to put down roots.

Jamie sighed and glanced over at the lifeguard's chair. Someone else was in it, and she wondered where Steve was. She looked around the beach and didn't see him anywhere, but she did see Rick, who was waving wildly and shouting Cindy's name.

"Cindy. I think your brother's trying to get your attention."

Finally, Cindy looked up. "Oh, my gosh, I almost forgot. I'll never know why, but I promised to go fishing with him and my father this morning." She jumped up and smiled at Todd. "Nice to meet you." Then she ran off.

Jamie wished Todd would run off, too. She wasn't angry with him anymore; she just wanted to get back to her letter. She could hardly write with his shadow looming over the page, though, so she turned back to him. "It really was a nice hike," she said.

"Good." Todd pushed the hair off his forehead. "That's what I wanted to talk to you about. I'm—I'm sorry I was so rude when you asked me to come. I didn't mean to be; I've just been a little . . . out of it lately."

Jamie was just about ready to ask why when she noticed a new pair of feet by her towel.

"Hi," Steve said.

"Hi." Jamie stood up, and so did Todd, so she introduced them.

"Listen," Todd said after he and Steve shook hands. "I'm going to get wet." He looked at Jamie. "How about some cannonballs off the pier?"

Jamie shook her head. "Not right now. Maybe later, okay?"

"Fine." Todd raised his hand to both of them and then left them alone.

"Hi," Steve said again.

"Hi." Jamie fished around for something else to say. "Have your muscles recovered?"

"What? Oh, from the hike, you mean."

"Yes." Jamie laughed. "My legs felt like they'd been pounded on when I got up yesterday."

"Umm. Well, I work out with weights a lot, so I'm in pretty good shape." Steve took her hand, and they sat down together. "I'm on duty in about five minutes," he said. "But I have a couple of hours off this afternoon. Want to do something?"

"Sure."

"Great. I'll pick you up at about three o'clock, and we'll go into Spruce." He squeezed her hand, got up, and trotted over to his chair.

Jamie watched him climb up, thinking that he certainly was in good shape, and then she went back to her letter.

To be continued!

* * *

120

"A date? With whom?" Mrs. Watson had just come back from the boat, and Jamie was helping her wrap the fish. They'd already been cleaned, so she didn't mind too much.

"His name's Steve," she said. She put the last trout in the refrigerator and grinned at her mother. "Are you ready for this? He's one of the lifeguards."

"Oh, my—a dream come true!" Mrs. Watson started to laugh and then stopped. "I'm sorry, honey. I didn't mean to make fun of it."

"That's okay," Jamie said. "I've been laughing, too." She started some water for tea. "I'm not complaining, though."

"I don't blame you. So. What's Steve like?"

"I don't know yet. He graduated from high school, but he has to work for a while before he can go to college." Jamie thought a minute. "I think he's lonely."

"Why?"

"Well, he's got all these jobs, and he doesn't have much time for fun." She grinned again. "Yet."

"Oh, that reminds me." Mrs. Watson got up and brought the kettle over. "I spoke to Todd's mother about the way you said he's been acting."

"Mother! I didn't want you to do that!"

"Don't get excited, please. It was a very confidential conversation." Jamie's mother blew on her tea and took a sip. "Alice didn't go into any detail, but she did say that Todd broke up with a girl about a week before they came here."

"Oh." Jamie figured that if Todd was so upset about it, he must have really been in love. Now she envied him *that*, too. "So that's what's bothering him."

"Yes, and not a word of it is to leave this cabin."

"Don't worry," Jamie said. "The only thing that's leaving this cabin with me is my old yellow tank top. And my last pair of jeans. They're all I've got left that's clean."

"Oh, no." Mrs. Watson set down her cup. "Your father promised to go into Spruce this afternoon and pay a visit to the laundromat, but now he's off with the Mitchells exploring some old broken-down fort. And I wanted to take some pictures. How come everybody forgets the laundry around here?"

"I'll do it," Jamie said. "Steve and I are going to Spruce. We can put the clothes in and then walk around town or something. See the sights."

Her mother laughed. "I thought you said you wanted him to have fun."

"So?" Jamie laughed, too. "You can have fun doing laundry. It all depends on who you do it with."

It felt odd, actually driving into Spruce. Jamie had always walked to the little town, and even now, when she had a license, it had never occurred to her to ask for the car. Steve didn't think it was strange at all, but then he hadn't spent nearly every summer in his life there, hiking in for comic books and bath soap.

The road was wide and easy to drive on, but it was still a mountain road. Signs told them to watch for falling rocks and crossing dear, and once when Jamie looked out the window, she saw a small herd of animals way off in the distance.

"Look!"

"I can't," Steve said. "There's a curve coming up." He kept his eyes on the road. "What was it?"

"Antelope, I think. Or elk. My parents would know." Jamie turned around to look again, but the valley had disappeared behind a hill. "They were running along and leaping around like they were playing a game." She laughed. "Maybe they're trying to stay in shape."

"Probably scared." Steve took a hand off the wheel and pointed toward the windshield. "See that copter? It must have spooked them."

Jamie saw the helicopter blades flashing in the sun. "I guess you're right. I'd rather think they were having a good time, though." She cleared her throat. "I know doing laundry probably isn't your idea of a good time. I hope you don't mind."

"No problem. Everybody's clothes get dirty." Steve turned to her for a second and smiled. "Besides, I like to meet people, remember?"

The Spruce laundromat was a clean, modern place, set around the corner from Taylor's Drugstore so that it wouldn't distract from the "rugged" atmosphere of the main street. It wasn't exactly a great place to meet people, though, so Jamie and Steve stuffed three loads of clothes into three different washers, then walked around the town. That took all of fifteen minutes, and Jamie was afraid that Steve might be bored as they went through the drugstore and the western shops. But he held her hand the whole time and seemed happy to be with her. He even took her on a quick tour of the restaurant where he waited tables every night. As he was showing her around, he made jokes about the tips he got.

"My parents only brought us here once or twice," Jamie said. "I think the last time was six years ago. They have a thing about 'roughing' it."

"You're not missing much," he said. "Not a whole lot goes on except the sounds of chewing." He took her hand and laughed. "I spend too much time here, anyway. Let's go."

Jamie had some postcards to mail for her parents, and Steve wanted to check his mailbox, so they went to the post office.

"Hey!" Steve said. "I got the ski-instructor job at Aspen. Looks like I'm set for the winter."

123

"That's great," Jamie said. "I've never been skiing there, but we drove through it one summer. It's beautiful."

"I'll bet. I'll bet it has more life in it than this place, too." He laughed again and held out a piece of paper. "And speaking of life, look at this."

Jamie looked and saw a flyer advertising "Cinema at 10,000 Feet."

"It's in a town called Rimrock," he said. "They've got an outdoor movie theater. Can you believe it? The guy at the desk said it's about an hour-and-a-half drive south of here." He put his hands on her shoulders. "What do you say?"

"About what?"

"About driving over there some night and checking it out." He ran his hands down her arms. "There's not much happening around here. What's an hour's drive?"

"An hour and a half?" Mr. Watson looked ready to bellow. "On mountain roads? At night?"

"Daddy." Jamie handed him a pile of clean, folded clothes and followed him into the bedroom. "Half the drive would be in daylight. And once we get out of Spruce, the roads are paved. It'd be like driving at home."

"That's what worries me." He stuffed the clothes into the rickety dresser and headed for the living room. "Anyway, you didn't come up here to go to the movies."

"Why not?" Jamie said. "We've been here almost two weeks, and I've done everything else there is to do."

"Except fish." Jeremy looked up from the fire he was building. "I haven't seen you on the boat or in the streams once. All you do is follow that lifeguard around."

"Give me time, Germ. The vacation's not over yet."

"Lifeguard?" Jamie's father poked at the fire. "You didn't say anything about a lifeguard."

"You didn't give me a chance." Jamie looked at her mother, who was fiddling with the camera. "Come on, Mom, help me out here. Please?"

Mrs. Watson sighed. "Jamie met a nice boy who happens to want to take her to a movie. I'm not crazy about the drive, either, Bob, but if you forget about the fact that we're in the mountains, it's like any other place."

"I suppose you're right." Mr. Watson sighed, too, and looked at Jamie. "Just be careful."

"I will, Daddy." Jamie laughed. "But I don't even know when his next night off is, so don't start worrying yet, okay?"

Steve's next time off, except for an hour or so here and there, turned out to be a lot further away than Jamie expected. First one of the lifeguards—Chuck—got sick, and it turned out to be appendicitis. He couldn't come back, and for a few days there was no one to replace him, so the other two lifeguards had to take his shifts plus their own. That meant Steve was working extra hours during the day plus his other jobs, so he and Jamie hardly had time to do anything but walk up and down the beach once in a while. Jamie told her father she'd let him know when to start worrying.

She spent a lot of time with the rest of the "Green's Peak Six," as they called themselves. Cindy and Rick were always ready to do just about anything, and M&M turned out to be really good at volleyball, so they played that a lot. Even Todd joined in once in a while. He still kept to himself quite a bit, but when he *was* with the rest of them, he wasn't terribly grouchy, and Jamie thought maybe he was beginning to come out of his slump.

Sunrise Lake didn't have horses, but Cindy and Rick discovered some stables at a ranch about an hour away. Jamie got permission to take the car by agreeing to let

Jeremy come along, and Todd got *his* family's car by taking Dave.

On the drive, Jamie kept wishing that Steve was there, but once they started riding, she almost forgot about him. She hadn't ridden much, but she'd been horse crazy since she was four. Nobody else sat a horse that well, either, especially Todd, and when they came to what looked like a shallow stream, she got a little worried that he was going to be a bad sport about it.

The rest of the horses walked to the edge and lowered their mouths to the water, but Todd's horse had a mind of her own. Before he could stop her, she plunged into the stream, which turned out to have a few deep spots. In two seconds, Todd was up to his thighs in ice-cold water. His horse looked perfectly happy to spend the rest of the day there.

Rick turned to Jamie. "Well, what do you think we should do?"

"About what?"

"About Todd," Cindy said. "He's cute, but he can be awfully touchy sometimes, if you know what I mean."

"I know what you mean." Jamie wanted to defend Todd, but there was no way she could do it without being a gossip.

"I say one of us goes in and gives him a hand," Matt said. "His legs are probably frostbitten already," he joked.

Jamie shook her head. "No, let's leave him alone. He can make it out by himself."

"I don't know," Mark said. "He's sure not trying very hard."

They all stopped discussing the situation and looked at Todd, who hadn't moved. But then he turned around, saw them watching, and grinned. "You know the old saying," he shouted. "'Your horse can lead you to water, but she can't make you drink!'"

Everyone laughed, and Jamie knew that Todd was ready to have fun again.

◦ *Five* ◦

Jamie was prowling around her room, trying to find something to read, when she noticed the notebook she'd been using to write Carrie's letter in. It was sitting in the exact same place, gathering dust, where she'd put it a few days before. She picked it up from the floor, blew on it, and opened it to the last thing she'd written—"to be continued." Her vacation was about half over, and she still hadn't finished the letter. She looked around for a pen, but once she found one, she realized she had nothing to write. "To be continued" said it all. She sighed and tossed the notebook on her bed.

"Mom?"

"What?"

"Have you seen my books?"

"I think I saw one of them in the living room. By the fireplace."

Jamie pulled the blanket back, headed for the fireplace, and found the book on top of the woodpile. It was supposed to be both a spine-tingling mystery and a sizzling romance. She picked it up and flipped through the pages. She could use some spine-tingling sizzle.

Her mother came in and stared at her. "What on earth do you want with a book in your hands? It's an absolutely beautiful day, and we won't be here forever, you know."

"I know." Jamie sighed again.

"You're not sick, are you?"

"No."

"Well, that's good." Mrs. Watson smiled. "How's your lifeguard?"

"Busy."

"Oh, so that's it."

"Umm." Jamie flopped down on the couch. "I was hoping we could be together a lot more. I mean, what's the point of having a boyfriend—not that that's what he is yet—if you can't be with him?" She held up her hand. "And please don't tell me that absence makes the heart grow fonder."

"I wasn't going to tell you any such thing. But maybe it's true. And maybe—what's his name?"

"Steve!" Jamie groaned. "See? Absence just makes the heart forgetful."

"It's not my heart we're talking about." Mrs. Watson sat down beside Jamie and patted her knee. "What I was going to say was maybe Steve feels the same way you do." She picked up the book and scanned the back cover. "Anyway, just because you can't be with him doesn't mean you can't have fun." She read a little more and frowned. "Where did you find *this*?"

"In Spruce. The drugstore had about ten copies of it and nothing else."

129

"No wonder." Mrs. Watson tossed the book aside. "As I was saying, if you're restless, don't sit around the cabin reading junk. Go out; breathe some fresh air. You might not get what you want, but at least you'll get tired, and then you won't have the energy to worry about anything."

Jamie decided to follow her mother's advice. M&M had become fanatics about volleyball, and she figured she might as well join a game and wear herself out. But when she got to the beach, everyone was gathered around the net, discussing baseball instead of volleyball, and Rick had an old, beat-up bat in his hands.

"Jamie, great!" he said. "That makes six of us."

"We're getting a game up," Todd said. "We can use you. Remember that flat place up behind the cabins?"

"Flat? You must have forgotten about all the fallen trees."

"That's okay," Rick said. "I never did like artificial turf."

As they started off, trying to decide on the rules for lopsided teams, Steve came running up beside Jamie.

"Hey," he said. "I've got a free hour. What's up?"

"Softball." Jamie was so glad to see him, she took his hand without even thinking about it first. "I'm glad you're here—now we can pick a permanent pitcher, and it'll be three against three."

"That's crazy," he said. "We'll spend most of our time chasing after the ball."

"Not if everyone hits like I do." Jamie laughed. "Come on; it'll be fun."

After a lot of negotiations, they divided up into two teams—Steve, Cindy, and Rick against Jamie and M&M. Todd volunteered to be the pitcher. "I don't want to brag," he said, "but I can get it over the plate three times out of ten."

Steve was right. There was a lot of running after the ball, since they had to play the bases and the outfield at the same time. Jamie was surprised by the way he played, since he'd seemed so reluctant to take part in such a makeshift game. But when they got started, he took it very seriously, she noticed. He cheered his team when they did well and practically took it personally when Rick tripped in a hole and didn't make it to second base.

Jamie was better at fielding than at batting, but on her sixth time up, with the score tied at ten, she got lucky and hit a really long ball. She made it past first and second without any problem, but as she headed toward third, she saw Cindy out of the corner of her eye, tossing the ball to Steve, who was waiting with his hands out. Jamie closed her eyes and dived for the base, which was a pile of pine needles that had to be reassembled every time someone slid into it.

She felt the pine needles scatter and jumped up. "Safe!"

"Out!" Steve scrambled to his feet and held the ball up. "Out by a mile!"

Jamie picked herself up out of the dirt and watched as Steve held out his arms and hugged Cindy. He spun her around and around, and Cindy looked as pleased as if he'd kissed her. Jamie thought of the time three summers before when Jim had spun her around after she'd done the mile swim, and she knew exactly how Cindy felt. She couldn't tell what Steve was feeling, but she couldn't help remembering the way he'd smiled at Cindy on the hike. If he was interested in *her*, why did he keep his arms around Cindy for so long?

She told herself he was just caught up in the game. She decided to get back into it, too. "I was safe," she said.

"Oh, no." Steve finally put Cindy down and ruffled her hair. "My outfielder here made a perfect throw. You just didn't feel the tag."

"She didn't feel it because it wasn't there," Matt said.

"Wait a minute; wait a minute." Todd strolled up. "I was watching, too, you know."

Everyone turned to him, and he grinned. "Except for a bunch of pine needles flying through the air, I didn't see a thing."

Jamie laughed and suggested they flip a coin. Steve wasn't thrilled with that idea, but he went along. Jamie won the toss.

"That's the highest-scoring game I've ever been in," Jamie said. She and Steve were walking back to the beach together. Her team had won by eight runs.

"It was all because of a bad call," he said. "I still say you were out."

Jamie laughed. "Come on, it wouldn't have made any difference."

"I guess you're right."

"Besides, it was just for fun."

He smiled and took her hand. "I guess you're right about that, too. It's just a game."

"Hey, Jamie."

Jamie put her finger in the pages of her book and walked across the porch. Todd was standing on the steps in his swimming trunks, a thermos in one hand and a towel in the other. He held up the thermos like a trophy. "Feel like rowing across the lake?"

"You're kidding."

"Nope. I woke up this morning, and somehow I knew that if I didn't go the distance today, I never would." He grinned. "Besides, after that fiasco with the horse, I have to do something to prove I'm not a total klutz." He pointed to her book. "You don't really want to read, do you?"

What Jamie really wanted to do was be alone with Steve long enough to find out who he was, but she couldn't tell that to Todd. "Well," she said, "it *is* a mystery."

"Come on, Jamie." Todd pulled open the door and waited for her to come out. "I know you better than that."

"All right." Jamie tossed the book into a chair and stepped outside. "But I warn you, I'm quitting at the first sign of a speedboat."

"You think I'm not?"

By the time they reached the boat, Jamie was glad to be out. If she couldn't be with Steve, she might as well enjoy herself some other way, and rowing across the lake and back would kill a couple of hours at least.

For some reason, she was sure that Todd would quit about halfway across, but even though he dog-paddled and complained a lot, he stuck it out.

"That's another name for the Sunrise record books." She reached out her hands and helped him into the boat.

Todd was grasping and rubbing his legs. "That's not why I did it."

"I know, I know." Jamie laughed. "You did it because it was there, right?"

"Wrong." He draped his towel over his head and took a long drink from the thermos.

"Oh, right," Jamie said. "The 'klutz' reputation—you wanted to get rid of it. Except it was the horse's fault, not yours. You must have made a bet with Dave or somebody."

"Wrong again."

"Well why, then?"

"I'm not sure." He peered out at her from his terry-cloth veil. "I just swam over a mile without knowing the reason." He shook his head and burst out laughing. "I must be crazy!"

"You think *you're* crazy?" Jamie pointed to a huge white blister on her left palm, but she was laughing, too. "I left a soft chair and a semigood book for this!"

They took turns rowing back, and as Jamie watched Todd drag himself from the boat and stagger up the beach toward his cabin, she was still laughing. She tied the boat up and was trying to decide what to do next when she saw Steve walking toward her.

"Hey, good news!" He put his hands on her shoulders, bent down, and kissed her on the lips. It was the first time he'd done anything more than hold her hand, and Jamie wasn't quite ready for it.

She pulled back, blushed, and then laughed, hoping she didn't look too embarrassed. "I can tell that," she said. "What's happened?"

"Chuck's replacement just got here. And I managed to get off from the restaurant. So . . ." He slid his hands down her arms.

"So . . . ?"

"So how about 'Cinema at 10,000 Feet'?" He bent down again but stopped short of kissing her. "One of the other guys says it doesn't really matter what the movie is. According to him, Rimrock really rocks. So why don't we find out if he's right?"

"Okay. When?"

"Tonight."

"Oh." Jamie frowned. "It's just that Cindy and Rick are leaving tomorrow. We're having a cookout and bonfire tonight on the beach. Sort of a big farewell." She smiled and let go of his hand. "It was my idea."

"Well, I don't know when I can get another night off." Steve looked a little impatient. "Come on, Jamie. That guy said it can really get busy, and there'll be a big crowd. I'm itching to get out of here for a night."

Jamie thought a minute and finally nodded. "Okay. Maybe we can get back in time for marshmallows, anyway."

"Great, so I'll pick you up about four." Steve was smiling again. "We'll have some fun."

Jamie leaned toward the wavy mirror and put some light blue shadow on her eyelids. Then she stood back and took a look. Blue eyes, blue eye shadow, blue cotton sweater, and blue jeans. Color coordinated but not too imaginative.

She wiped off the eye shadow, went back to her room, and changed into a pair of oatmeal-colored Indian cotton pants. They were more comfortable, anyway, and if she couldn't be comfortable on the inside, she might as well try for it on the outside.

In the kitchen, her father was sitting at the table, eating an apple and looking glum.

"What's wrong, Dad?"

"It's windy. It's cloudy. It might rain."

"Oh. Not very good fishing weather, huh?"

Mr. Watson looked at her. "Not very good driving weather."

"Daddy." Jamie kissed him on the cheek. "Don't worry. I'll be fine." She took a bite of his apple. "If you really don't want me to go, I won't." She couldn't believe how hopeful she sounded.

"No, no." Her father shook his head and patted her hand. "You go and have a good time. I even promise not to pace the floor."

Jamie kissed him again and went out on the porch to wait for Steve. It was almost four o'clock, and she couldn't figure out why she wasn't counting the minutes.

She finally figured it out at five after four, and once she did, she was surprised it had taken her so long.

135

Steve was hardworking and good-looking and reasonably nice—she couldn't argue about that. But he wasn't particularly serious, at least not about her. She knew that Cindy was right; she didn't have to be in love to have a good time, but that made her think of something else— she and Steve just didn't "click." He was in one of the most beautiful places in the world, but he didn't really see it. He'd rather drive to some "in" town where there'd be lots of other people than be alone with her. And another thing. If *she* was really in love, she'd be happy just to take a walk. But she knew she wasn't in love. And since he wasn't, either, she also knew she'd have a better time at the beach with her summertime friends than with some boy who didn't really care about her.

Two hours later, as Jamie walked along the beach toward the fire, Cindy spotted her and shouted, "Jamie! I thought you weren't going to be here!"

"Well, here I am, anyway." Jamie laughed and held up four wooden legs. "One of our kitchen chairs finally broke down, so it's my contribution to the bonfire."

"Good, we can use it." Rick handed her a stick with a hot dog on it. "Let's eat first and then really build a blaze!"

Todd and the twins were scouting the beach for pieces of wood, and while Jamie toasted her hot dog, Cindy came up beside her and whispered, "What happened? I thought you were going to the movie with Steve."

"I was," Jamie said, "but I changed my mind."

"Oh, I hope you didn't feel like you had to be here. I understood, you know."

Jamie laughed. "I know. I just decided I wanted to be here, that's all."

"Oh." Cindy looked confused. "You didn't have a fight or anything, did you?"

136

"No, nothing like that." Jamie had been a little worried about breaking the date at the last minute, but when she told Steve that she'd decided she wanted to stay at the beach, he didn't put up much of an argument. He asked why, and when she said she thought she'd have a better time at the party, he was surprised. He didn't kiss her, of course, and Jamie figured he wasn't going to be paying that much attention to her from then on, but she was just as glad. She didn't really want his kisses.

"We didn't have a fight." She looked at Cindy and grinned. "I just decided to throw him back in the lake."

Cindy burst out laughing. "*Now* you do it! When I'm leaving tomorrow!"

The bonfire attracted a lot of attention, and by the time it was at its height, the little farewell party had grown by about twenty people, all armed with their own marsh-mallows and ready to sing at the top of their lungs.

Jamie's parents strolled over. Her father looked relieved that she was on "safe" ground, she noticed, and her mother looked relieved that she wasn't acting heart-broken. Jamie laughed to herself. She was far from brokenhearted—she was having a great time.

⚘ *Six* ⚘

"*I* wish somebody'd tell me why it's always so important to get an early start," Cindy said. Her hair was the only bright spot in the 5:30 A.M. gray light.

Rick blinked at her like an owl. "You didn't complain when we went to Green's Peak."

"Yes, I did," she said. "The rest of you were just too sleepy to hear me."

"Well, you can nap in the car, at least." Jamie tried to laugh, but it turned into a yawn. She'd only been out of bed ten minutes, just long enough to pull on some clothes and trot over to Cindy's cabin to say good-bye. She shoved her hands into her vest pockets and wished the sun would hurry up.

Cindy's parents were over at the main cabin, returning their key and paying up. The car was all loaded. "I wish you weren't going," Jamie said. "What am I going to do

138

for the next three weeks?" It sounded selfish, but it was true. Even though she and Cindy weren't close friends, she'd still miss her company.

"Let's see," Rick said. "You already swam the lake. There's always volleyball."

"*Please*. Don't even mention volleyball."

Cindy perked up a little. "Maybe some other cute guy will come along."

Jamie smiled, but it was too early in the morning for boy talk, for *her*, anyway.

They stood there a few more minutes, yawning at each other, and then Jamie spotted their parents hurrying back. She turned to Cindy. "Good luck with the cheerleading."

"Thanks." Cindy shivered and hugged her.

Jamie waved as they drove away. Then she started back to her cabin. But halfway there, she realized she was wide awake. She turned off the path and headed toward the water.

It was almost six, and it was one of the few times she'd seen the place at that hour of the day. The sky was getting lighter, and she could see three or four people already heading for their boats, hoping to fool the sleepy fish with shiny lures.

She passed by the lifeguard's chair and looked up. It was empty, of course, but she decided that for her it always had been. She tried to figure out how she felt about it all; she even tried to be sad, but the most she could come up with was a slight feeling of disappointment. It would have been wonderful if Steve had turned out to be the love she was looking for. He hadn't, but at least she was finally finished with *that* fantasy.

She stepped onto the pier and looked down at the water. The sun had finally made it over the hills. The lake was changing from black to blue again, and the air was starting to warm up. Jamie opened her mouth and gave a huge, jaw-cracking yawn. She obviously wasn't as awake as she thought. She might not know what she was going to do for the next three weeks, but she knew exactly what to do now.

"Jamie?"

"Umm." Jamie rolled over to her back, opened her eyes, and blinked at the brand-new beige ceiling.

"Jamie."

"What?" She propped up on her elbows as her mother came into the room. "What time is it?"

"Almost ten-thirty."

"Oh, my gosh." Jamie flopped back down. "I can't believe it. I slept for four hours."

"Well, don't spend too much time stretching and burrowing," Mrs. Watson said. "Todd's here."

Jamie yawned. "What's he want?"

"I don't know." Her mother slung the camera around her neck. "I'm on my way out right this minute, and he's waiting on the porch, so don't fall asleep again."

"I won't."

After her mother left, Jamie swung her legs over the side of the cot and sat for a minute. Then she realized that she hadn't even bothered to take off her clothes when she'd come in.

She stuck her head into the kitchen, yelled, "I'll be right out, Todd!" then changed into some fresh clothes, brushed her teeth, threw some water on her face, and went out to the porch. She still felt groggy and wrinkled. "Hi."

Todd was standing at the screen, wide-eyed and wide awake. "Hey, Jamie, come on. I've got something to show you."

"What?"

"You'll see when we get there."

140

Jamie tried to yawn with her mouth closed and failed. "Where are we going?"

"Just a short hike." He pointed to her bare feet. "It's not a rough trail, but I'd advise you to wear shoes. And bring some apples or something, okay? We might get hungry."

"Why didn't you bring them? You planned this, whatever it is."

"I know, I know. I just forgot a few details. Oh." He looked at her. "I forgot. Maybe you'd rather be at the beach." He didn't say any more, but he looked slightly embarrassed, and Jamie could tell he was thinking of Steve. It was the first time he'd shown that he'd even noticed her and the lifeguard.

She shook her head. "No. Cindy and Rick left this morning, and I'm not in the mood for volleyball. Or swimming, either, right now." She didn't want to come right out and say that everything was over between her and Steve, but she felt that she had to say something. "So . . . there's no reason for being at the beach."

Todd nodded as if he'd gotten her message, then grinned. "Well, come on, then. Aren't you curious?"

Jamie padded back inside to get her shoes. Todd was excited about something, and he was probably building it into more than it was, as usual. But at least a walk would clear her head, and besides, she *was* curious. She put some apples and a bag of Oreos into her duffel bag and followed him out the door and into the woods.

Todd walked very fast and kept talking to her over his shoulder. "I was up at eight this morning, and everybody else had plans but me, so I decided to take a walk. Hey, Jamie, did you ever fly over the mountains?"

"No."

"I did once. My aunt died in California, and we flew out for the funeral. It was in September, and you wouldn't

141

believe the way the aspen trees look then." He pointed to one of them, which was still a pale green. "From the air they're like huge pools of gold in the forest."

"They sound different then, too," Jamie said. "Sort of dry and scratchy, but nice." The Watsons had an aspen in their backyard, but she knew they didn't grow in Kansas, where Todd was from. "They really quake in the fall."

Todd kept talking about leaves and trees and birds, and Jamie was beginning to wonder if he'd brought her out for a nature walk when she finally woke up enough to notice where they were headed.

"Uh, Todd, this doesn't have anything to do with Tyler's Ghost, does it?"

He turned around and tried to look innocent. "What makes you think that?"

"Oh, maybe because we're on the trail that leads right to his cabin."

"Clever, Jamie." He laughed. "Well, it does have something to do with it, but we're not going to the cabin. Have you been to it this summer?"

"No."

"I have." He kept on walking.

"Well?"

"Well what?"

"Well, is it still the same?" Jamie hadn't gone because she still felt mortified every time she thought of the last time she'd tried to get to it, but she couldn't help wondering.

Todd laughed again. "Exactly the same. Right down to the tin pots."

Before they reached the cabin, he veered from the main trail and took another one that sloped down to the lake's edge. "Almost there," he said.

142

Jamie was really getting curious, and she followed him without asking any more questions. He stopped right before they reached the water, disappeared into the undergrowth, and then came back out, carrying something in his hands.

"What is it?" Jamie said.

"Look."

She took it from him and looked. It was old and rusty. Some of the metal fell away in flakes as she held it, and as she turned it over, she burst out laughing. "A lantern! An old, falling-apart lantern!" She looked out at the water. They were standing at the bend in the lake, where she'd always seen the bobbing light. "But this can't be it," she said to Todd. "This couldn't possibly shine anymore."

Todd put on his old Dracula accent. "But don't you see what this means, my dear? The ghost walks no longer. The ghost is dead, ha-ha!" He dropped the accent. "The ghost is dead."

He looked happy and sad at the same time, and Jamie had a funny feeling that he was talking about somebody else besides Ben Tyler. She wasn't sure, though, until Todd sat down and looked at her. "I'm sorry, Jamie, about the way I acted when I first got here."

"That's okay."

"No, it's not." He twisted a leaf in his fingers and frowned at it. "I acted like a complete jerk."

"Well, not a complete one."

"Thanks." He smiled and took a deep breath. "Anyway, there was this girl. I thought we were really tight, you know? But it turned out we were as far apart as . . . I don't know." He glanced up at her. "Anyway, do you remember that night we sneaked out and came over here?"

Jamie sat down, too. "How could I forget?"

143

"On the boat, remember? I was telling you how I was a little scared of girls—of getting into that ball game because I wasn't sure I could play it?"

"I remember."

"I still don't know how."

Jamie cleared her throat. "I'm not so sure it's a game."

"You're right." Todd stopped shredding the leaf. "It's not a game, but some people treat it like one, and I have a problem doing that."

Jamie cleared her throat again. "And this girl wasn't...serious?"

"No," Todd said. "I guess she wasn't the love of my life, but she was for a while, and when it was over, it hurt." He looked around for something else to keep his hands busy and started peeling the bark from a twig. "Jamie, did you ever want something so bad you tried to fool yourself into thinking you had it? Even though you knew deep down you didn't?"

"Yes." Jamie knew he was talking about love, and she thought of Steve and even Jim. "And when you stop fooling yourself, it hurts." She wasn't sure what else to say, but Todd didn't seem to expect anything else. He was back on his feet again, examining the lantern. Finally, he tossed it back into the bushes and dusted his hands.

"So..." He grinned at her and pushed his hair back. "What song are we going to sing?"

"I don't know." Jamie started laughing. "I thought maybe you'd figure a way to get us out of it."

"Oh, no." Todd was laughing, too. "You're the one who got us into it, so weaseling out of it is up to you. But just in case you can't manage it, we'd better have something to fall back on."

Jamie took out the apples and some cookies, and as they headed back, they ate and tried to think of a song that wouldn't make them sound too ridiculous.

"How about something in two-part harmony?" Todd suggested.

"Harmony? Todd, I'm lucky if I can stay on key."

"Ah, yes, it's all coming back to me now."

Jamie threw a cookie at him, and they watched a squirrel scamper down a tree, sniff it, then reject it.

Jamie picked up the cookie and suggested "Oh, Susannah," but Todd turned that down because it had too many high notes.

By the time they got back to the lake, they hadn't agreed on what to sing, but they were still laughing.

Jamie was glad that Todd was "back" again, especially since Cindy and Rick were gone and Steve might as well have been. It was amazing how quickly Steve disappeared from her thoughts even though he was still around. They waved and said "Hi" to each other, and Jamie decided there weren't any hurt feelings, because there hadn't been any real feelings between them in the first place.

It was fun to "play" with Todd again. They spent most of their time together, swimming, hiking, playing volleyball with M&M. They even went snake hunting once, but when they found one, they were both too scared to go near it. "I'm beginning to think you get cowardly as you grow up," Todd said.

Being with Todd was fun, but now there was something different about it. Jamie wasn't sure what. Maybe it was because they'd shared something more than snake hunting—because they'd talked about love and agreed that the whole thing was baffling. Or maybe it was just because they were older and really couldn't "play" the way they used to.

But she began looking forward to seeing him waiting for her on the beach or hearing him yelling through the screens for her to come on out, and it wasn't until the vacation was nearly over that she finally figured out what had changed between them.

She'd gotten up early, but Todd, who usually got up earlier, wasn't heading down the path toward her cabin, and he wasn't anywhere on the beach, either. She trotted back to the Mitchells' cabin, smiling at the thought of tossing pebbles at his window and waking him up.

The cabin's inside door was closed and locked. The Mitchells' station wagon was gone. Then Jamie remembered Todd's saying something about his family taking a drive farther up the mountains to some old mining town that Dave had been begging to visit again. Since they were busy climbing rocks when he told her, she hadn't listened very carefully, but that day must have been the day.

She walked back to her cabin, got her sizzling mystery, and took it to the beach with her. She read for half an hour and finally realized that the book was never going to sizzle. No wonder there'd been so many copies of it left.

Jeremy and her father asked her to come fishing, but she wasn't in the mood for it. Her mother came by and suggested swimming or a hike, but Jamie didn't feel like doing those things, either.

She plugged along in the book, trying to find the mystery, and every once in a while, she'd glance toward the cabins to see if Todd was back yet. By four o'clock, he still wasn't, and Jamie figured they must have decided to make a whole day of it and then stop somewhere along the road for dinner.

The book didn't sizzle, but her skin was beginning to, so she picked herself up and ambled back to the cabin. That night, after losing three straight games of Monopoly to Jeremy, Jamie yawned and stretched. "I think I'll go to bed."

146

Mrs. Watson looked up from her book. "It's only eight o'clock."

"Is it? It feels later." Jamie shrugged. "Well, maybe I'll shower first, then read in bed."

"You're not sick, I hope."

"No, I'm not sick," Jamie said. "How come every time I do something you don't expect, you think I'm sick?"

"Jamie." Mr. Watson spoke softly, so she knew he was annoyed. "Your mother just asked a civil question about the state of your health. Try to be just as civil when you answer."

"I'm sorry." Jamie sighed. "I'm not sick. I'm just a little tired. I'll be fine tomorrow."

She took a lukewarm shower because her skin was burning, then drowned herself in lotion and got into bed.

She tried to read, but the book really was a waste of time. Her notebook, with its unfinished letter to Carrie, was still on the floor, and the sight of it made her feel guilty, but not guilty enough to get up and do something about it.

She lay back on the bed and stared at the ceiling. It was quiet outside, as usual, and she kept listening for the sound of the Mitchells' car. When she heard it, she smiled and closed her eyes, picturing Todd at the wheel. He hated to drive, he said, but his parents just assumed that he loved it, like most teenagers. He made Jamie promise never to tell anyone about that.

Jamie smiled again, then opened her eyes and sat up. That's what had been wrong with the day—Todd hadn't been there. She'd missed him, and not just because he was somebody to do something with, either. She'd missed *him*.

❋ *Seven* ❋

The minute Jamie opened her eyes the next morning, the thought of Todd came marching right back in and pushed everything else out, including the pain in her sunburned shoulders. She'd gone to sleep thinking about him, then woke up thinking about him, just the way she'd done three summers before with Jim. Her feelings for Jim had been real enough, but they weren't made to last. The way she felt about Todd was different; she'd decided that before she fell asleep. With Jim, she'd imagined all sorts of impossible situations—dancing on the beach, gliding across the lake under the moon. With Todd, she knew she'd be happy just to put on her boots and work up a sweat hiking around the trails. Not that she'd mind a romantic situation, complete with moonlight, but all she really wanted was to be with him.

No, that wasn't all she wanted. She wanted him to want the same thing, for the same reason. Falling in love with her summertime buddy was the last thing in the world she'd expected to do, but since she had, she decided to accept it. The only problem now was Todd.

"Jamie? Are you awake?"

"Yes."

"Good." Jamie's mother stuck her head around the door. "Todd's here."

"He is?" Jamie blushed, but she knew it wouldn't show, so she didn't care. "Well...tell him I'll be out in a few minutes, okay?"

"Sure." Mrs. Watson smiled. "You certainly look rested. You must have slept well."

"I did." Jamie laughed. "I slept better than I have in my whole life."

She took some clothes from her closet and went into the bathroom, trying to figure out what to say to Todd. Absolutely nothing came to mind. She pulled on some shorts and a blue-green knit top that left her shoulders bare. If she couldn't say anything, the least she could do was look good. She tried to ignore the tomato color of her nose and put on a little eye shadow. She thought about the lemon splash but decided it would sting too much. She took a last look in the mirror, a deep breath, then went out to the porch.

Todd was sitting in one of the chairs with a fishing rod beside him and his rubber high boots on. He stood up when Jamie came out and squeaked a few steps toward her. He looked wonderful.

"You look like a lobster," he said. Then he cackled. "You should do as the count does, my dear, and sleep when the sun is shining." He squeaked back to the chair and picked up his fishing rod. "Dave told me about your bet with Jeremy. I know for a fact that you haven't landed a single fish yet, so how about trying to catch up?" He pointed to a paper bag on the chair. "I even brought food this time."

Jamie walked back inside, put on some jeans and a sweatshirt, wiped the dust off her pole and boots, and followed him out the door. In forty-five minutes, she was thigh deep in a cold stream, stumbling over rocks and feeling the sweat starting to smear her eye shadow. So much for looking good.

She kept trying to think of things to say, but it wasn't easy. All of a sudden, she wasn't good at talk, small or otherwise. She knew why, of course; she just hoped Todd didn't notice that she'd suddenly lost her tongue as well as her heart.

She looked back and watched him for a minute. His hair was really bleached now, and she kept wanting to push it off his forehead, just to know what it felt like. She thought of all the times they'd been together, all the times their hands had touched when it never meant anything. Now, when it would have meant everything, he was standing fifteen feet away from her, watching his line as if it were the only thing on his mind.

He started reeling it in then, and Jamie looked at it. This time, she knew exactly what to say. "Todd! Where's your hook?" She looked again. "You don't even have a lure or anything. How do you expect to catch any fish that way?"

"I don't." He waded down to her and tried to look sincere. "See, I . . . ah . . . I didn't want to ruin your chances."

"Come on!" Jamie didn't have any trouble touching him then, either. She gave him a shoulder punch and laughed when he almost toppled over. "I don't believe that for a minute. The only thing you're better at than I am is skipping rocks over the water."

"I know, I know." Todd cast his hookless line again. "Okay, here it is. I like to swim and row and hike and all that. But Jamie, I just don't like . . . catching things!"

Jamie laughed even harder. "Well, *I* didn't really feel like fishing today either, if you want to know the truth."

He stared at her. "Then what are we doing here?"

"I don't know."

"I don't know, either." Todd pointed toward the bag he'd left on the bank. "So let's eat."

Jamie finally managed to find some words, and even though they weren't the ones she really wanted to say, the picnic was fun. They both ate until there was nothing left, and on their way back to the cabins they decided to tell everyone who asked that the fish just weren't biting.

"You must have been in the only place where they weren't," her father said that evening. "Your brother and I were tempted to go over our limit."

"Oh, well, I guess we just weren't lucky." Jamie poked at her salad. She'd loved being with Todd that day, but now that she saw him differently, just being with him wasn't enough. She wanted to share what she felt, but she didn't know how. It made her restless and edgy and definitely not hungry. She took the last forkful anyway, so nobody would make any comments about her being sick.

Her mother immediately passed her some more. "What are your plans for tomorrow, Jamie?"

"I don't know. I'll have to check my calendar," she joked. "Why?"

"Well, your father and I thought it would be nice if we—all of us—got away from the lake for a day. I know Jeremy's getting a little stir crazy."

"That's for sure." Jeremy frowned at his food. "Dave said the mining town was great. Could we go there?"

"We went there last summer, remember?" Mr. Watson leaned back in his chair. "But I was talking to some people, and one of them told me about another place. It's a

151

ghost town, but it's all fixed up now, so you can pan for gold and ride a stagecoach, and I think there's even an old train that takes you around."

Jeremy perked up. "Sounds great!"

"Sounds tacky to me," Jamie said.

"Oh, come on, Jamie." Mrs. Watson laughed. "Don't be such a purist. It'll be fun."

"I'd really rather not go." Jamie tried to sound casual. "How about if I stay here and have dinner ready when you get back?"

Mr. Watson shook his head. "No, this place is a three-hour drive away. We'll want to spend a lot of time there, and who knows? We might decide to find a motel so we don't have to drive back late at night."

"We're not sure about that part yet," Mrs. Watson said. "But just in case, we don't want you to spend the night here alone."

Jamie nodded. What could she say? "But I want to be with Todd"? It was the truth, but it wasn't anything she was ready to tell her family.

She wished she could let Todd know where she'd be the next day. Three years before, it would have been the most natural thing in the world for her to go over to his cabin after dinner and explain why she wouldn't be around. But now she was so afraid he wouldn't care where she was that she couldn't make herself do it.

She was glad, though, when Jeremy raced over to invite Dave. It turned out that he had a bad cold and couldn't come, but at least Jamie knew that Todd would know where she was the next day, whether he cared or not.

Fool's Gulch was exactly what Jamie had expected—a tourist trap that sold popcorn and sacks of fool's gold and even staged a high-noon shoot-'em-out between the sheriff and an outlaw. The only exciting thing was a ride, which Jeremy insisted they all take, straight up the side of a mountain in an open mining car. Jamie forgot about Todd for the first time that day and concentrated on not getting hysterical when the car stopped halfway up. She felt like a fly on a wall, except that she didn't have any wings and the "floor" was about thirty feet down.

Her parents and the Germ had a great time, and Jamie had a feeling that she would have, too, if Todd had been there. She smiled every time she thought of the comments he'd make, and she knew he'd really love panning for gold, whether it was real or not.

She also knew that in spite of what her parents had said, they had no intention of spending the night in a motel when they had a perfectly good cabin waiting for them at Sunrise Lake. She was glad when they got back about nine o'clock. All day she'd tried not to think of Todd, and all day she'd failed, so it felt good knowing she was at least near him again. She thought it would make her sleep better.

She couldn't sleep at all. Sitting in a car for eight hours usually made her more tired than hiking or swimming, but not that night. Finally, at about ten-thirty, she sat up, put on some jeans, a heavy sweater, about three pairs of socks, and tiptoed out to the porch. The cold air would probably wake her up even more, she thought, but she hated lying in bed waiting for sleep to come.

She was standing by the screen, staring out across the lake, when she heard a noise outside and almost shrieked. She started to make a mad dash back inside when she heard a "Psst!" and forced herself to turn around. "Todd?"

He was outside, at the far end of the porch, his nose mashed up against the screen, peering at her like an owl. "Sorry I scared you," he whispered. "Our garbage can was full. I decided to use yours, since Dave conveniently came down with a cold and passed the job on to me."

Jamie's knees finally stopped shaking, and she managed to walk across the porch. "Aren't you scared of bears?"

"Terrified." He put his hands on the screen like a prisoner, and Jamie laughed.

"Want to come in for a minute?"

In two seconds, he was up the steps and inside. "Thanks. I'll just take a second to get my courage back, and then I'll be on my way." He sat down slowly so that the chair wouldn't squeak. "What I need is the bear scare to carry with me. I could shake it and keep everything away."

"And wake everybody up." Jamie laughed softly. "Anyway, it's missing."

"You're kidding." He looked disappointed. "Now we'll never catch a bear."

"We can always build another one," Jamie teased.

"Right. Let's get started tomorrow." He grinned. "How was Fool's Gulch?"

Jamie told him all about the place, and Todd immediately wanted to go and pan for gold, just as she knew he would. It was chilly outside, and she kept trying to keep her teeth from chattering, but she didn't want to leave until he did.

When she finished describing the day's outing, Todd yawned and apologized.

"That's okay," she said. "It *is* a little late."

"True. But my courage is only beginning to return." He grinned again. "What were you doing out here, anyway?"

"Oh, I—I just couldn't sleep." Jamie thought fast. "So I decided to look for the lantern." She stared out across the lake again. "I didn't see it, though."

"I thought we agreed." The chair creaked a tiny bit as Todd got up and walked across the porch. "The ghost is dead."

"We did," Jamie said. She felt him close behind her. "But it's kind of fun to look."

"I know. Jamie?"

"Yes?"

"I missed you today."

Jamie turned around. "You did?"

"I did." He took a step closer and pushed the hair from his forehead. "You didn't really think I braved bears and bobcats just to bring the garbage over here, did you? I mean, I did, but I guess I . . . just wanted to . . . to see your car and know you were back." He smiled. "How's that for courage?"

Jamie looked down at her triple-socked feet. Then she decided that was a dumb thing to do, since everything she wanted was right in front of her. She looked up and into Todd's sparkling dark brown eyes. "I missed you, too," she said.

When they kissed, Ben Tyler's ghost could have marched right past the cabin, and neither of them would have noticed a thing.

❋ *Eight* ❋

Dear Carrie,

Forget about the lifeguard, because I already have. Something's happened that you won't believe, and I hardly can, either. Read the part about Todd the Grouch and then get ready!

Pebbles rattling against her window screen made Jamie stop writing and scramble to her feet to look out. Todd was standing outside. The way she felt toward him now, she almost expected to see him on a beautiful horse, waving a plumed helmet at her. Instead, he was wearing sneakers and waving a brown paper bag, but he was smiling like a prince. "You ready?" he said.

"For what?"

"A picnic."

Jamie peered down at her travel alarm. "Todd, it's seven in the morning. Nobody's up."

"I am. You are." He shifted back and forth on his feet to keep warm. "I think it's a perfect time for a picnic. What about you?"

"You're right." Jamie laughed. "I'll be out in five minutes."

She dressed in a hurry, brushed her hair and teeth, scribbled a note for her parents, and tiptoed outside. Todd held his hand out, and she took it. Their hands fit perfectly; she'd never noticed that before.

They walked a little way without talking, and finally Jamie said, "Where are we going?"

"Just wait." The path was still wide enough for them to walk side by side, and Todd put his arm around her waist. "You look great, considering the time."

"Thanks, I think."

"Sorry." He stumbled over a tree root and laughed. "I guess I'm not too smooth."

"I don't mind a bit." Jamie laughed, too, and missed his arm when the path narrowed and he took it away to walk ahead of her. "Where are we going, anyway?"

"To Tyler's cabin. Okay?" He glanced back at her. "I thought we should take one last look."

The cabin was still there, just falling apart a little bit more. Whispering as they'd always done, Todd and Jamie crept up the path and stopped outside the door. He squeezed her hand and pushed it open. Spider webs brushed their faces as they stepped inside and looked around.

The fireplace, the tin pots, and the old blanket were all still there, covered with dust but there. Jamie looked at Todd and grinned. "Maybe the ghost isn't dead after all."

"Well, if he's not, he's going to have company for breakfast." Todd let go of her hand, found enough twigs

157

to last for about half an hour, and started a small fire in the crumbling fireplace.

In a few minutes, they were sitting next to the low flame, eating oranges. Suddenly, Jamie laughed. "If anybody notices the smoke coming out of here, they're going to get a real scare."

"Maybe." Todd dropped their orange peels into the paper bag. "But I've got a feeling it's only the little kids who keep the myth going."

"Like we did," Jamie said. "But Todd, how do you explain the pots and pans and stuff? The place is falling apart, but it's so . . . tidy. Even the chimney isn't blocked."

"Well, I've got a feeling about that, too." He scooted closer to her. "Remember the last time we came here together and found the bread wrapper?"

Jamie nodded and put her head on his shoulder.

"And your brother said that guys brought their girlfriends here." Todd laughed. "Well, no guy would bring his girl here if the place were covered with mold and too dusty to breathe in. So they keep it . . . tidy."

Jamie laughed, too. "I didn't believe it then. At least I didn't want to." She turned her head and looked at Todd, who smiled and kissed her softly. "I believe it now," she said.

They sat together until the fire died out completely. Then they decided to go back, have a real breakfast, and go swimming.

Right before they left, Todd wadded up the bag and stuck it in a corner of the fireplace. Then he grinned. "Let's leave something for somebody else to wonder about."

Later that day, Todd had plans to row the boat for Dave, who wanted to try to "go the distance," so Jamie decided to hike into Spruce and mail Carrie's letter.

As she left the post office and started back, she was thinking how surprised Carrie would be and how much they'd have to talk about when she got home, even though the letter probably wouldn't get there before she did. That's when it hit her. There was so little time. She and Todd only had a week left to be together. She'd found out she loved him just about the time she'd have to leave him.

She took her time getting back, trying to tell herself that even though they lived in different places they could still write. And if the Mitchells came back the following year, they could have another summer together. Then she remembered that would be the summer before she and Todd started college and they might both have jobs. Maybe they could figure out a way to get together before the following summer. Or maybe they could even go to the same college after they graduated. Things were getting very complicated, and by the time she reached the lake, she had a headache from thinking about it.

She spotted Todd in the boat not too far from the pier, and she figured that Dave still had a long way to go, so she headed back to her cabin.

"Mom, do we have any aspirin?"

"It's in the bathroom, where it always is." Mrs. Watson looked up from the new laces she was putting in her boots. "Don't tell me. Let me guess—you're lovesick, right?"

Jamie smiled, went and took the aspirin, and came back into the living room. She hadn't told anyone about Todd, but she should have known her mother would notice. "I guess it's pretty obvious, huh?"

"Well, I think it may have escaped your brother, but anyone over the age of twelve couldn't miss it." Mrs. Watson laughed and stood up to give Jamie a quick hug. "I think it's lovely, Jamie. Todd's a wonderful boy."

"Yes, he is."

"Then why do you need aspirin?"

159

Jamie sat down by the fireplace. "I just realized that . . . Mother, do you think it's possible that Todd and I will keep loving each other even after we're apart?"

"Honey, I don't know. You and Todd might keep in touch, and who knows? In ten years, you could get married. Or you could keep in touch and fall in love with other people." She finished lacing her boots and smiled. "But I think if you really love each other now, then you probably always will, in some way."

Jamie figured her mother might be right, but it was so "iffy." She didn't want an "if"; she wanted an "absolutely." She knew she couldn't have that, though, and it made her restless.

She changed into her swimming suit and decided to do some laps between the pier and the raft while she waited for Todd. After fifteen minutes, she knew exactly why he had done laps when he first got to the lake. They wore you out so much you couldn't think of anything but your muscles.

She did a few more, then climbed onto the pier and wrapped a towel around her. In a few more minutes, Todd and Dave came back. Jamie watched as they tied up the boat. Todd gave his brother a pat on the back and then trotted over to her.

"Hi." He sat down beside her and dangled his legs over the edge of the pier.

"You look wiped out." Jamie laughed. "Did he make it?"

"Nope. Poor kid." Todd glanced back at Dave, who was trudging up the beach. "He's still so skinny; his arms are like spaghetti. Now he thinks he's a failure."

"What did you tell him?"

"I told him he'd do it next year, for sure. If we come back."

"Oh." Jamie stared at her toes and sighed.

"What's the matter?"

"What you said about next year and coming back." Jamie took a deep breath. "Todd, we only have a week left."

"I know." He took her hand. "I've been thinking about it, too."

"It's kind of sad, isn't it?" Jamie said. "Who knows what's going to happen after—after we say good-bye." She tried to laugh. "We'll write, won't we?"

"Of course we will." Todd squeezed her hand. "That doesn't solve the problem, though, does it? I mean we can't see into the future."

"No, I guess not."

"I wish we could," Todd said. "I bet it's going to be beautiful."

"You do?"

"Mm. No matter what happens." He looked at her. "I love you, Jamie. If we've only got a week, then let's make it the best week of our lives."

Jamie didn't know if it would be the all-time best week of her life, but she knew for sure that it was the best so far. She stopped worrying about what would happen and started enjoying what *was* happening.

She and Todd were together as much as possible— rowing, hiking, eating hamburgers in Spruce, and cannon-balling off the pier. They were the same things they'd always done, but for Jamie, they felt completely different. The summers before, she'd enjoyed Todd's company because it was all she had. Now she enjoyed it even more, because it was all she wanted.

Jeremy finally noticed the obvious, and he went out of his way to tease Jamie whenever he got the chance. "Now that you're in *love*," he said in front of the whole family one morning at breakfast, "you walk around humming to yourself all the time. Doesn't it bother your boy-friend?"

Mr. Watson laughed. "Jeremy, you talk about love as if it were a disease."

"I don't hum in front of Todd, anyway." Jamie smiled at her brother. "We have better things to do."

"Must get pretty boring, holding hands and staring at each other."

"Just wait, Jeremy," his mother said.

"For what?"

"Until it happens to you."

"Right." Jamie leaned across the table. "Remind me to ask you how bored you are then, Germ."

Jeremy's face went beet red, and he had to gulp some milk to recover. Then he grinned. "Well, there's one nice thing about it. Now that you're in *love*, you'll never catch enough fish to beat me. I bet that was the last time you ever call me Germ."

"I certainly hope so," Mrs. Watson said.

"Maybe it was," Jamie said. "But I've been thinking about it. You know, Jeremy, it's the quality that counts, not the quantity."

"So?"

"So how about if we start fresh? We'll have a sort of onetime shot at it, and whoever lands the biggest fish wins."

Jeremy shook his head. "That wasn't the deal."

"I know, but it'd be more fun, wouldn't it?" Jamie said. "I mean, I haven't caught a single fish all summer. I haven't even tried. What fun's a contest without an opponent?"

"Yeah, but it's awfully chancy," Jeremy said.

Mr. Watson smiled. "Don't ever tell anybody I said this, but fishing is mostly luck."

162

"I bet I can do it, anyway," Jamie said. "I'm feeling like a winner."

"Oh, because you're in *love*." Jeremy sat back and shook his head at her. Then he laughed. "Oh, who cares? I'm going to beat you, anyway, even if you are cheating by changing the rules. You're on, Jamie."

They shook hands on the new deal, and later that morning Jeremy and Dave got in one boat, Jamie and Todd got in the other, and they rowed out to the middle of the lake for the big fish-off.

"I hope you don't mind," Jamie said to Todd. "I don't really know why I'm doing this, except he kept on bugging me and I let it get to me." She lowered her voice. "Don't worry. You don't have to fish."

He laughed. "I don't mind helping you. You don't think I'd stand on the beach when I could be out here alone with you, do you?"

Jamie looked around. Except for the other boat, they *were* alone. It was a beautiful morning, and she was with Todd. She cast her line in, then almost forgot about it.

Todd pulled the oars in and let the boat drift. "Thought of a song for the cookout yet?"

"No." Jamie smiled. "My mind hasn't been on it."

"I've thought of a million," he said, "but they're all love songs."

Jamie leaned across and kissed his cheek. "What's wrong with that?"

"Hey, Jamie!" Jeremy was standing in his boat, pointing to the fish he'd just caught. It looked about six inches long. "The next one'll be bigger!" he shouted.

Jamie waved and turned back to Todd. "Now, what's wrong with a love song?"

"Nothing. I love love songs." He took her hand and grinned again. "I just can't sing them."

"Neither can I." Jamie laughed. "Okay, let's do 'Clementine.' That's your mother's favorite, anyway. And it's short."

"Good point." Todd sat back. "Come on, we've got to practice."

They both started singing, very softly at first, but after a minute they were singing as loud as they could and laughing even louder.

"Hey, you'll scare the fish!" Dave shouted.

"No, we're serenading them!" Todd shouted back. He opened his mouth to sing some more, but nothing came out. Finally, he pointed. "Jamie, look!"

Jamie didn't have to look. She'd already felt the tug on her line. "Oh, my gosh, I think it's big!" She started to reel. "It feels like a whale!"

"Easy, easy. Take it slow." Todd scrambled around in the bottom of the boat for the net. "Maybe the line's just snagged."

"No, it's a fish; I can tell," Jamie said, and started to laugh. "I don't believe this."

"Don't laugh; you'll lose it."

"Right, right." Jamie pulled and reeled and tried not to laugh, and in a few minutes she'd landed her first fish of the summer. They both stared at it for a second.

"Well, it's not a whale," Todd said. "But it sure is big. I have a feeling Jeremy just lost."

Jamie nodded and glanced over at her brother. He was standing in his boat, and even though he couldn't see the fish, he looked really excited. He was all caught up in the situation.

"I think he deserves to win." She bent down, quickly unhooked the fish, and tossed it back in the lake. Then she shouted, "Too small, *Jeremy*!"

* * *

Two days later, Jamie and Todd sang their "duet." They got through it without breaking up, but then everybody insisted that they sing it again, because it was so short. Jamie didn't mind. She didn't want the night to end, because it was the last one. There was no way she could hold back the stars, though, or keep the moon from climbing higher, and at five-thirty the next morning, she walked over to the Mitchells' cabin to say good-bye. All night she'd been trying to think of things to say, but when she got there, her mind went blank.

Todd finished helping pack the car, then took her hand and led her a little way down the path.

"This isn't easy," he said.

Jamie nodded and leaned her head against his chest. "I warn you, I might cry."

"I might, too."

They put their arms around each other and stood close together for a minute, bumping foreheads. Jamie pulled her head back, then reached up and pushed at his hair. "I've been wanting to do that for a long time."

Todd smiled. "This isn't easy, but I wouldn't have missed it."

"Neither would I."

Todd kept his arms around her and kissed her softly. He didn't say good-bye; he just turned and walked back up the path. Then he stopped and waved.

Jamie raised her hand and waved back. She listened ɔr the car, and when she couldn't hear it anymore, she knew he was gone.

She stood alone for a few minutes, thinking. Todd was gone, and she really didn't know for sure if they'd ever be together again. And even if they were, she didn't know if it would be the same. But she did know she loved him and that she always would, in some way.

She shivered and started back to the cabin. She didn't have to pack, but she'd help out, anyway. With Todd gone, she didn't want to stay behind a minute longer than she had to, and she couldn't wait to get going.

Conclusion of Book Two

Author Carol Ellis remembers her fourteenth and seventeenth years....

"When I was fourteen, I worried most about the way I looked—not constantly, but I don't think a day ever passed that I didn't wish I was beautiful.

"The summer I was fourteen, my family moved to a new city, and I spent the months before school started hating my new home and trying not to be terrified about starting in a new school.

"There was a boy on a bike that summer—blond, and probably blue-eyed, although I never got close enough to see—who delivered the paper to our house every afternoon. Seeing him was the highlight of my day and I waited for 4:00 P.M. the way I used to wait for Christmas. Sometimes I planted myself on the porch with a book, or moved the sprinkler around the front yard, just so I'd be outside when he rode by, but I never exchanged a wave with him, let alone a word. Nevertheless, by the time school started— we were practically in love—in my imagination—much like Jamie's fantasy about Jim, the lifeguard.

"When I was seventeen, I was still dissatisfied with things, but I didn't retreat to my room or to my imagination quite so often. I auditioned for and made the lead in a school play, and dated a good-looking popular boy.

"If I'd realized at fourteen that I could make good things happen for me, I probably would have waved to that paperboy."

Carol Ellis lives in New York with her husband and young son.

From 14 to 17

For a Young Girl, There's an Eternity Between

From freshman to senior year, girls go through lots of changes. In the *Heart to Heart* series, each novel tells two stories—about the same girl—at the age of fourteen; then at seventeen. In each, we see her struggle, change and grow.